The Triumph Of My Soul

EDITED BY ELISSA GABRIELLE

Peace In The Storm Publishing

Praise for The Triumph of My Soul

"*The Triumph of My Soul* takes you on a journey, beyond the masks and facades we create in our "perfect little world" and forces us to move from relying on our own abilities to total trust in the Father."

~Wanda B. Campbell,
Author, *First Sunday in October*

"Awesome, heartfelt and inspirational read. These incredible short stories will make anyone who may be going through a family crisis, abuse, health problems, heartbreak and whatever life dishes out, to feel a sense of relief, uplift and awareness. These stories prove how important faith in God is."

~Tinisha Nicole Johnson, Author of *Searchable Whereabouts*

"What a testament of faith and the Grace of God. These stories moved me to tears...tears of joy!"

~Diane Dorce'
Author, *52 Broad Street*

"Inspiration is generously offered through the written words of each contributing author of Triumph of My Soul. Within its pages we become acquainted with an immutable truth; that truth being that He will never leave nor forsake us. It is a work that will most assuredly cause its readers to reflect upon their past and present views on life."

~Dr. Linda Beed
Author, *Business Unusual*
Co-Host, Faith Based Arts Conference

"The Triumph of My Soul is a testament of the power of the spirit and prayer in our daily lives. Through these authors, we repeatedly see how God "shows up and shows out." It can be illness, death, depression or lack of worldly goods; if you take His hand and let faith lead you, nothing can stop you. This book is uplifting for the mind, body and soul."

~Sydney Molare', Author

"Often we find ourselves feeling as though we just can't win for losing. In *The Triumph of My Soul,* readers will find that they are not alone. This is more than just a book of short stories; you have been given a personal invitation to share in a journey. You will laugh, cry, and be utterly amazed by what these authors and/or their characters have had to conquer. Most importantly, you will be inspired to rise above your circumstances and press forward. Treat yourself and experience *The Triumph of My Soul.* You will be better for it."

~Janet West Sellars, Author of *Quiet As It's Kept* and the forthcoming, *Can't Let Go.*

"Thought provoking, and inspiring. *The Triumph of My Soul* reminds readers that no matter what obstacles you face, you're never alone."
~Lacricia Peters, author *Girl, Naw!*

"Many times in life we face disappointments and pain. As women, feel alone because we learn early on who our friends are as we battle our self esteem issues. *The Triumph of My Soul* gives us hope as we are reminded we are never alone! God is always present."

~Minister Nicole L. Warren
Vashti School for Future Leaders

FOREWORD

God speaks through our trials. Through Him, we find peace in the storm. Say that to yourself three times. Peace in the storm. Now, meditate upon the thought of souls finding tranquility in the midst of turmoil; it can be challenging, uplifting, and victorious at the same time. *The Triumph of My Soul* will enlighten your senses, feed your spirit, and nourish your soul with encouraging stories about faith, hope, love, redemption and inspiration of the human spirit.

You will take a journey into the hearts and minds of the storytellers and their characters and find spiritual rejuvenation. A successful writer must possess several natural abilities like perception, discernment, conception, imagination, and the will to be self critical. Sometimes one must respond to harsh disappointment, reject some opinions and accept others. Sometimes one has to navigate opposites to walk together through difficult situations in unison from time to time. A genius is one who can make those things happen. These storytellers demonstrate their genius in how they've incorporated a wonderful, everlasting message of conveying the awesome glory of God.

You will discover the joy within through these inspiring stories of victory over adversity with the turn of each page. You will laugh, cry, be moved and motivated to positive change. Walk away from this experience knowing that whatever tribulations you may face, whatever challenges comes your way, God loves you always. There are no trials that you cannot handle. Enjoy the triumph because it is worthy of reading and all who do so will say, "It was well worth my time."

Grace & Peace Always,

Elissa Gabrielle, Publisher
The Triumph of My Soul

CONTENTS

Julian's Grace
Jessica Tilles

In a heated rush, traffic barreled up and down Georgia Avenue, NW, in Washington, DC, going nowhere too fast. Julian Winters stood before the bay window, peering through the blinds, wishing he were amongst the traffic, escaping the sterilized smell that caused his stomach to flip about like a fish out of water. This wasn't one of his favorite days, but none of them had been lately.

"Life wasn't meant to be lived so hurried," he fussed between clinched teeth. "But then again, it's short as hell."

Pressing his palms against the cool windowpane, he lowered his head, desperately trying to suppress the inner pain. After all, spending so much time at Howard University Hospital, was difficult for him. As much as he wanted to scoop her up from her sickly bed and fly away to a destination where cancer didn't run rampant, he knew it was impossible and the inevitable was around the corner.

As he raised his head, he slowly opened his eyes and gazed up at the clear blue sky, challenging his once strong faith in God. Daily, Julian questioned God, not knowing what He was trying to prove by taking away the most precious life that meant the world to him. Was it something he did in his past to build anger in God? As far as Julian was concerned, God must have been harboring anger toward him and taking his beloved Grace was his punishment. All his life, he felt God was a forgiving God, so why couldn't He forgive Julian of his past sins, whatever those were?

"Sweet Heavenly Father," he prayed silently. "I'd give my life for Grace's."

He wasn't ready for her to go; he needed her there with him. There was still so much love and life to live with Grace. After fifteen years of marriage, he was still learning about Grace Winters, and each day brought on a different Grace, lively and intriguing. She never failed to amaze him. It was Grace's intent, from the first day she laid eyes on Julian, to keep the spice in their lives until death did them part. And she kept her word.

Too weak to toss and turn, she was having a good dream, although it was receding quickly. Her nose twitched at the familiar scent of Joop, forming a smile on her face. It was her favorite, and Julian always wore it for her. She stretched her eyes open and looked around the room until they landed on Julian's once strong statute. *This has taken such a toll on him*, Grace thought as she admired his broad shoulders that had permanently slouched.

An exhausting sigh escaped her. "What are you doing, fussing again, honey?" The soothing soft, angelic voice came from behind him.

A smile graced his face, for her voice was sweet music to his ears, a melody all her own, to never be replicated or duplicated. One he would have to get used to living without.

"You want slow pace, move to Idaho," she softly chuckled, followed by a gut-wrenching cough.

With his back to her, Julian cringed at her cough. "Are you okay?"

She cleared her throat. "I'm fine, honey. How are you this morning?"

Turning to face the love of his life, Julian's smile was wide as a piercing blue ocean and as bright as the sun. Walking over to the bed, he stood motionlessly, all the while maintaining the smile, although forced, that Grace loved so much. He didn't want to be there and, above all, he didn't want his wife to be there.

"I thought you would never wake up, Gracie. I'd be better if you weren't in here. How are you feeling, sweetheart?" He gazed down at her as if seeing her for the first time, mesmerized by her beautiful baldhead and ashen pale complexion. Although he deeply missed her flawless pecan hue and flowing honey blonde ringlets that used to dance about her forehead—swiping them away from her face was the sexiest thing he'd ever seen—she was still beautiful in his eyes.

Grace tilted her head to the side and turned up the corner of her mouth. "Hmm. Fair to midland, I suppose."

Julian reached for the chair that sat against the wood-grained double closet and pulled it up beside the bed. Sitting, he leaned forward, resting his upper torso on the edge of the bed. Clasping his hands together, he smiled, puckered his delectable lips and blew her a soft kiss.

Palms stretched open wide, happily she grabbed at the air, clutching his kiss, rather weakly, in her hand. Her strength had dissipated; she could hardly hold an ink pen between her tiny fingers. Slowly, and with shaky limbs, she brought his kiss up to her lips and savored it. Smiling, she closed her eyes and cringed a little from the pain that shot throughout her being.

"What's wrong, Gracie?"

She pursed her lips and gave two shakes of her head.

"Are you in pain, honey?"

"I'll be okay, Julian." She patted his hand. "Sweetie, how long have you been here?" Her voice was weak and faint, soft like cotton, barely above a whisper.

Not confident in her assurance, Julian clasped her hands in his and lowered his head before responding. "Not long…about an hour. You were sleeping so peaceful. I didn't want to wake you."

"I appreciate you not waking me, honey. I've been poked and prodded all night long. The only time I can rest is during the day actually."

"Well, I've taken the rest of the afternoon off. So, you have me all to yourself."

"Wonderful! I've been missing you like crazy too."

"Sweetness, *I'm* the one who is missing *you* like crazy." He gently shook his head. "The house isn't the same anymore. It feels strange without your presence. It's too quiet."

"Honey, please don't do this to yourself."

Tears welled in his eyes and danced on the rim, before diving down his cheek and streaming over his chin. He was so torn up; he felt it difficult at times to control his emotions in front of Grace.

"What am I supposed to do, Gracie…live life without you? I can't do that." He jumped to his feet, slightly kicking the chair, swinging in mid-air in anger. "I just can't do that!" With his back to her, he tried so hard to be strong for her, not letting her see him break. However, he was finding it very difficult to maintain. The woman he'd loved more than his own life was dying. Day after day, he prayed for God to take him, and spare his Gracie. Feeling helpless was too much for him. *Damn it*, he thought.

Wrapping his arms around him, he hugged himself tight and lowered his head. "Oh, Gracie, how can I manage without you, babe?" From deep within, he pulled out a cry that was silent but felt deep in his heart. He's supposed to be the strong one with her being so weak. However, the tables have dramatically turned. She's dying and he doesn't have the power to rectify her status. He'd never felt more useless in his life. He vowed to be her protector and he failed.

Grace tried to pull herself up in the bed by grabbing hold of the railing, but she didn't have the strength. She fell back onto the pillow.

Admiring the weakness exuding from Julian, Grace smiled and made a feeble attempt to calm him. "Sweetheart, I know what you're going through. But," she sighed, "we have to accept reality for what it is."

"I just can't—"

"You have no choice, Julian."

He walked toward the bed and fell, lifelessly, down into the chair. Restlessly, he slumped forward, plopping all of his weight onto the bed resting his head on her stomach.

She stroked his black, thick curly tresses and coddled him. "There, there, baby. Everything is going to be all right."

He sobbed uncontrollably; silent cries like that of a wounded animal escaped him.

"Sweetheart," she continued, "Listen to me." She raised his head and stared into his hazel eyes, speckled with flecks of brown and pain. "I have come to terms with my fate. You should do the same. I love you. You have been a wonderful, loving and devoted husband—given more than I could ever dream of—and my heart is full, and…well, I'm tired, Julian." Her eyes broke the gaze they held with his and roamed around the room, landing on the window. "I'm tired of fighting a losing battle. I suppose, I could reminisce on all of the things I could have done different, but what is the use?"

Julian focused in on her soft brown eyes—so serene, patient and comforting—her eyes always calmed him during the most trying times.

With the back of her hand, Grace wiped the tears from his face.

"You're ready to leave me?"

"I'll always be with you." Again, she combed her frail fingers through his hair. "You know, I have no regrets, except one."

"What's that?"

"I regret that I was never able to give you a son."

He smiled and shook his head. "Your unselfishness amazes me."

"Love is not selfish, Julian."

Julian rose from the chair, walked over to the sink and splashed water on his face. "Thirsty?"

She stretched her arms above her head. "Yes, but I am *dying* for a Pepsi." Grace cracked herself up, as she fell out into a wicked giggle. "Get it baby, *dying*?"

Turning off the spigot, Julian snapped, "Don't say that!" Although he felt it wasn't funny, he wished he had her strength and endurance, and ability to make light of something so devastating.

Grace smiled and felt it unnecessary to respond. She didn't know of any way she could ease his pain. Her passing was inevitable, and this much he knew, but accepting it was the hardest thing he'd ever had to do. She accepted it and she hoped he would too, but she realized it was asking too much of a man who loved his woman more than he loved himself, let alone anything or anyone else.

"I'll go to the cafeteria and get you a Pepsi."

"Thank you, sweetheart."

Julian smiled. "Anything else I can get for you?"

Grace shook her head no, closed her eyes and sighed.

As Julian's hand wrapped around the door's handle, Grace opened her eyes and stared at his back. He sensed her piercing glare.

Glancing over his shoulder, tears flowed and glistened down his face.

Seeing Julian in such pain was killing her more than the cancer. However, she knew that once she was gone, he'd be fine. Or would he?

"A bag of Doritos, please."

Julian nodded. "I'll be back."

"I'll be here." She reached for the handheld apparatus to administer a quick injection of morphine.

❧ ❧ ❧ ❧ ❧

Julian walked by the hospital's gift shop, heading toward the cafeteria. He stopped abruptly. The pink stuffed elephant caught his attention. Grace absolutely loved elephants, no matter the color. However, since, she is a loyal member of Delta Sigma Theta, a *pink* elephant wouldn't do.

"She would kill me," he chuckled to himself as he imagined the look on her face if he gifted a pink elephant. His silent chuckle turned into a hearty laughter. It seemed like months since he laughed and it felt good, even though he felt guilty for doing so.

Entering the gift shop, Julian approached the counter and asked if the pink elephant came in red.

"What you see is all that we have, Sir." The elderly, white-haired volunteer clerk smiled widely. "The pink is beautiful though."

"Yes it is. I'll take it and a few crossword puzzles too, please."

The clerk returned with the items. "Can I get you anything else, Sir?"

Julian looked around and spotted the glass-encased refrigerator. "Oh yes, my wife is *dying* for a Pepsi." Smiling at his words, he tried to do as Grace would want—coming to terms with the inevitable—although it was hard as hell to do. He felt emotions rise in his throat and lodged at his Adam's apple. He swallowed hard, trying to hold back the tear that forced its way down his cheek. Quickly he wiped it away and rifled through his wallet. "How much?"

The clerk looked at him. Her heart ached for him. Unfortunately, it wasn't anything new. She'd seen his kind before, day after day. *Poor thing*, she thought, *if only men could be as strong as women.* "Thirty-two dollars and fifteen cents."

Handing her a twenty, a ten and three crisp dollar bills, Julian grabbed the elephant and white plastic bag with the Pepsi and crossword puzzles. "Thank you. Keep the change."

Leaving the gift shop, he walked toward the lobby and took a seat in the row of waiting room standard burgundy leather chairs facing the Patient Information desk. He buried his face into the plush stuffed elephant and cried softly for a while. He then gathered his composure, doing away with the tears, before returning to Grace's room.

ॐ ॐ ॐ ॐ ॐ

The door opened to Dr. Lockett standing over Grace's bed, with his two fingers and thumb pressed against her wrist, checking her pulse.

Julian stood still, searching his face for anything indicating a change in his wife's condition. He refused to give up hope.

"Are you resting comfortably," Dr. Lockett asked Grace.

"Yes," she sighed, "as much as I can."

"I know it's hard to rest when your vitals are being checked every hour," he chuckled.

Julian walked toward them. He placed the elephant at the foot of the bed.

"Wow, honey, they didn't have one in red?"

Julian smiled and shook his head. "Nope and I asked too. I guess you'll be an AKA for a while."

"Never!" she blurted out with laughter.

Julian turned toward Dr. Lockett. "So, how is my Queen, Dr. Lockett?"

"She's doing just fine," he smiled.

The sullen look on Julian's face turned into a hard frown. "No, she's not doing *just fine*. She's *dying*, doctor." His anger spewed out between clinched teeth, with poisonous venom. "How dare you make light of it?"

Grace called out to Julian a few times, but her calls were ignored.

"My wife is dying!" He slammed the bottle of Pepsi down on the movable table that stood beside the bed. "I wish you wouldn't act as though everything is so peachy keen!"

"Julian, please! It's not his fault."

Julian psychotically paced the floor. "No? Then whose fault is it?" His arms flailed in the air.

"It's no one's fault, sweetheart. Please calm down. I can't take too much more of this, Julian."

"My wife is dying and there isn't a damn thing I can do about it!"

Dr. Lockett understood Julian's anger all too well. He lost his wife to ovarian cancer five years ago. "Mr. Winters," he hesitated.

Julian faced Dr. Lockett, and folded his arms, arrogantly, across is chest. "What? You're going to tell me that you know how *I* feel?" His voice was filled with sarcasm.

Grace's calm demeanor had subsided. "Julian, damn! All of this is working my nerves. I'm dying and the *last* thing I want is people around me arguing over the inevitable. So please, do me this one favor...shut up!"

Julian faced her in disbelief. The woman who had been so meek, timid and sweet throughout their marriage is telling him to shut up. A smile graced his lips. He looked toward Dr. Lockett. "My apologies, doctor."

"It's no problem, really. And, I do know how you feel, Mr. Winters. I lost my wife five years ago to ovarian cancer. I am a doctor and couldn't save my wife's life. I was helpless and weak. She was strong as an ox," he faced Grace, "much like your wife."

Julian lowered his head. He felt like a complete fool, for he felt as if he were the only man in the world who was experiencing intolerable gut-wrenching pain.

"Well, I need to get back to my other patients. Mrs. Winters, please don't hesitate to let the nurses, or myself, know if you need anything, anything at all."

Although she was quite upset, her smile remained warm and comforting. "Thank you. I'll keep that in mind."

She waited for Dr. Lockett to leave the room before directing an annoyed look in her husband's direction.

"I'm sorry, Gracie. Don't be mad at me."

The wrinkles in her face softened. "Yeah, yeah," she smiled. "Where is my Pepsi?" She reached for the bottle of Pepsi and unscrewed the top. She closed her eyes, slightly tilted her head back and grazed her lips with the mouth of the bottle, feeling the coolness against her dry chapped lips. She parted her lips and allowed the ice cold Pepsi to seep through, swooshing around her mouth before flowing down her throat. She slowly gulped, feeling cold liquid flow down her chest and into her shrinking stomach, before swiping the back of her hand across her now pale thin-pursed lips. "That was so good," she said, between a couple of good hearty belches.

Julian laughed and took a seat at the foot of the bed.

She sat the half-empty bottle of Pepsi on the movable bed table and, with as much strength as she could muster, pushed it to the side. "Honey," she whispered.

Julian looked up and into her eyes. "Yes."

"Where are my Doritos?"

"Oh, sorry, Gracie, I forgot."

"It's okay. Do you remember the first time we met?"

"Yes, I remember." Taking her hand in his, he kissed each finger. "I thought you were heaven sent then and I still do."

With her free hand, Grace reached for his face and stroked his cheek. "You always did know the right things to say."

"That happens when you're speaking the truth, Gracie."

Missing the softness in his face, she smiled at him.

Julian slightly chuckled and leaned in to kiss her on the lips. "I love you," he cooed, rubbing his warm nose against her cold one. The warm breath oozing from his slightly parted lips warmed her insides.

She shivered.

"You cold?"

"A little bit. My temperature is dropping." She spoke without an ounce of concern.

"Stop it, Grace."

"I'm sorry."

"It's okay," he sniffed. "Now what were you saying about the first time we met?"

Feeling the strength slowly drain from her, she managed to whisper, "I want you to love me one last time."

Closing his eyes tightly, he shook his head and poked out his bottom lip. "Baby, I want nothing more than to love you. If loving you is going to keep you here with me, then I will love you with all my might, and as hard as I can."

Julian stood up from the chair and, with the back of his legs, pushed it across the room in frustration, where it bounced off the wall. Gently, he pulled back the covers and admired her fading beauty, as he lifted her hospital gown up over her stomach.

Quickly, she lowered the gown and turned her head to the side.

"What's wrong, Gracie?"

"I'm ugly."

"No you're not, honey." He leaned down and passionately kissed her lips. Then he pulled back and stared into her beautiful brown eyes. "You are the most beautiful woman in the world."

Once again, he raised her gown above her stomach and caressed her thighs, softly touching and caressing, moving upward and over her frailness, as he rose to the occasion. He wanted so badly to love her, and mesh with her one last time. He would give his soul to feel her being, storing it in his memory for years to come. Yet, she was too frail and his six-foot, two-hundred-fifteen-pound frame would crush her.

"Oh, Julian, you've always known how to make me feel good," she cooed, with closed lids and a satisfied smile on her face, her lips turned up into the most sexiest smirk he'd ever seen. "I would give anything to feel you one last time."

"Sweet, sweet, baby," he whispered, as he brushed his lips against hers. "I want so badly to be inside you, but I don't think it's a good idea, honey."

"Why not?" Her voice cracked, a soft cry welling in her throat. "You don't want me anymore, Julian?"

Leaning back, he smiled and adored her eyes. "Woman, don't be silly. I'm about to bust; I want to be inside of you so badly. But–"

"But, what?"

"But, I don't want to hurt you."

"You could never hurt me, Julian. Please, make love to me one last time. I'm begging you."

"You never have to beg me for anything, sweetheart."

With his hands propped on his hips, he contemplated the possible consequences of his pending action. Lowering his head, he realized he would hurt her more by denying her. Unbuckling his belt, he unzipped his pants and allowed them to fall to the floor.

Grace giggled.

"What's funny?"

"Suppose a nurse comes in and catches us."

"It will be much more exciting. Shall we call one in so we can get this party started?"

Grace laughed aloud. "You have no sense at all." She smacked him on the arm. "Now mount your Philly and get to riding, *Big Daddy*."

"Now you know that turns me on!"

Julian gently climbed on top of her and Grace parted her ocean. As his missile aimed for her sweet target, steadily he guided it, head first, into her abyss, careful not put too much weight on her.

A soft moan escaped her. "I love you so much, Julian."

Burying his face in her neck, he cried internally.

ىە ىە ىە ىە ىە

The following morning, Grace woke to Julian sleeping in the chair, under the window. Smiling, she reminisced on the previous night, and every kiss Julian planted was forever sewn on her body, stitched into her skin.

Feeling chilly, she pulled the crisp white blanket under her chin and silently cried. She felt herself saying a silent prayer, something she hadn't done since she was a child.

Grace's faith diminished at the tender age of twelve, when her mother died in a vicious car accident. It was then when she determined that there was no such God.

"Dear God," she paused. Blinking several times, before she thought of the next words that followed. "I'm sorry for not reaching out to you for so long. But, I was so angry at you for taking my mother away from me." She looked over at Julian. "I suppose much like how Julian's feeling now. I'm sure he's angry too, God, but please forgive him and help him to cope and live through this all. It hasn't been easy for him and it's only going to get worse." Wiping away the captive tear that escaped down her cheek, she took in a deep breath and slowly blew it out between her lips. "I know that in your mansion, there are many rooms, God, and I'm hoping you've prepared one for me. I promise I will get to know you again, before I come to live with you."

The morning shift nurse entered the room, interrupting Grace's private moment with God. "Good Morning, Mrs. Winters. How are we feeling this morning?"

"We are feeling fine, thank you."

"That's good," she said, placing her breakfast tray on the table. Looking over at Julian, "Can I get him a blanket?" she asked.

"That would be nice of you, thank you."

Retrieving the hospital-regulated blanket from the top of the double closet, the nurse placed it over a peacefully sleeping Julian.

"Okay, so is there anything I can get for you, Mrs. Winters?"

"Yes, if you don't mind, could you please get me a Bible?"

The nursed turned up her lips and smiled. She'd never received such a request. "Sure, I'll see what I can do. Okay?"

Grace smiled and nodded. "Thank you. I'd like to get to know my God before he sends for me, which will be soon. So, if you could make it quick, I'd really appreciate it. I don't have much time."

Peeking over at Julian, who was still fast asleep, she mustered all the strength she could and pulled herself up in the bed. After a brief pause, to gain her breath, she swung her legs off the bed and scooted her bottom to the edge.

Hearing her move about, Julian woke and sat straight up in the chair. "Gracie, what are you doing?"

"Oh, nothing, I'll be fine."

"Sweetie, let me help you."

"I'm okay, Julian."

Julian jumped to his feet and rushed over to her side. "I'll help you. What is it you need?"

"I want to get down on my knees."

"Why do you want to kneel down on this cold floor, Gracie?"

She jerked away from his grasp. "If you're not going to help me, then go sit down!"

"Alright, calm down. Here," he said, reaching for the pillow and dropping it to the floor, "use the pillow."

On her knees, Grace leaned against the edge of the bed and placed her hands together. She closed her eyes. "Pray with me, please, Julian."

Every emotion housed by his body had forced its way from the pit of his stomach up to his throat. He couldn't speak. He placed his hands together and closed his eyes.

"Our Father, who art in heaven," Grace softly prayed. "Hallowed be thy name. Thy Kingdom come." Julian cleared his throat and prayed with his wife. "Thy will be done, on earth as it is in heaven. Give us this day our daily bread. And forgive us our trespasses, as we forgive those who trespass against us. And lead us not into temptation, but deliver us from evil. For thine is the kingdom, and the power, and the glory, forever and ever. Amen."

Folding her arms before her, Grace lowered her head and rested in peace. Her prayers were answered. God forgave her and called her home, where she will bask in one of the many rooms that He prepared especially for her.

Opening his eyes, Julian wiped away the storm of tears and looked over at his beloved Grace.

"Gracie," he called out to her. "Honey," he gently shoved her by the shoulder. "I love you, Gracie."

Wrapping his arms around her, he lifted her, cradling her in his arms, savoring their final embrace, and laid her on the bed. The floodgate of emotions opened as he said goodbye to his soul mate, the love of his life and best friend.

"I'll see you soon."

MARATHON
Bill Holmes

Alex's recurring nightmare began at the starting line of the 1600-mile run. The hot sun was beating down on the athletes and the spectators with its ferocious intensity at Franklin Field. The excitement of competing at the Penn Relays increased every time he participated in this event. This year was no exception as anxiety permeated throughout his body. Bobbing his head and pacing back and forth, he cleared his mind of all thoughts and focused his attention to the sound of his cleats digging into the track. That would be the only noise he would hear for the next four minutes. His chest expanded slowly to the last breath he inhaled before taking his place at the starting line along with the other participants. Clenching his fists in anticipation, the starter's instructions became mumbled until he aimed the gun in the air, pulled the trigger and Alex took off with reckless abandon down the track along with the other runners.

Stay strong and don't lose focus, Alex thought trailing behind in second place. The first lap flashed by quickly as he increased his pace while keeping his eyes on his lanky opponent's feet. He dashed like a cheetah pursuing its prey when he effortlessly glided into first place halfway through the second lap. The roaring crowd's approval became oblivious while he directed his energy and concentration into maintaining his lead.

You did it, boy, now all you gotta do is stay sharp, he thought as he made his way around the curve to complete his third lap. That was when he felt his feet getting wet and soaked. He stopped running, looked down and noticed blood saturating his sneakers. A sharp pain sliced into his right leg as Alex approached the finish line. Screaming in agony, he fell onto the track while the other competitors passed him. The entire stadium slowly metamorphosed into the scorching desert terrain of an Iraqi city under siege from enemy forces. American soldiers and Iraqi civilians were running for their lives as ammunition and explosives erupted from all directions. The pungent smell of gunpowder and smoke filled the dusty air while Alex rose gingerly to his feet. Searching for shelter, he turned to his right, took a step and felt the force of a devastating eruption, catapulting his body thirty feet into the air until he awoke from his sleep.

"No!" Alex screamed, grasping for his missing right leg.

"What?" Cynthia, Alex's wife, shouted.

He shook his head and sat on the edge of the queen sized bed. His copper forehead and white cotton tee shirt were drenched with perspiration.

Cynthia leaned her body against the brass headboard, reached over and touched his shoulders. "Honey, are you alright?"

"Yeah," Alex replied, trying to catch his breath. "I'll be fine."

"Do you want to talk about it?"

"No," he answered. Reaching across the dresser, he assembled his prosthetic leg and walked out of the bedroom.

Cynthia glanced at the clock on her nightstand displaying the time 2:23 AM. She pulled the covers over her shoulder and sighed. She attempted to fall back asleep, but her thoughts won't allow her. Her eyes dampened, recalling the change in her husband's demeanor after losing his leg and his subsequent return home from Iraq. Gone was the loving Alex Mitchell she married for better or worse that was full of vigor about life. He could lift her spirits whenever she felt depressed with a simple, gentle hug or a soft kiss on her cheek to make her feel special. Alex barely displayed his affection anymore since coming home. The last time they shared a kiss was the day he left for deployment. Whenever they did embrace, his touch was so cold and barren, making her feel repulsed and unwanted. The man she was living with was a complete, silent stranger who kept his thoughts and feelings private. The toll was taking its effect on her marriage and she didn't know how much more she can bear.

The sound of the doorknob turning slowly broke Cynthia's train of thought. She remained motionless; listening to Alex's every movement until he climbed back into their bed. She felt him pull the cover over his body, lying beside her never saying a word. Slowly, Cynthia mentally counted to ten before she opened her mouth.

"Is everything okay?" she asked.

"Everything is fine," he replied nonchalantly.

"Are you sure? If you want to talk about what's on your mind, I'm here for you."

"Nothing is on my mind, Cyn. Please go back to sleep."

"Don't tell me to go back to sleep," Cynthia said, turning to face Alex. "We need to talk."

Alex stares at the ceiling. "About?"

"About you. About us," she answered, turning Alex's face towards her. "Look at me when I'm talking to you!"

He stared at her face and took notice of her full lips, furrowed brow and pleading, brown eyes. He removed her hand and said, "We'll talk in the morning."

"This can't wait!" Cynthia yelled, getting out of bed and picking up her husband's prosthetic leg. "We need to talk about this! We need to talk about what this is doing to you and to us!"

Alex stood up. "What are you doing? Put that down!"

"Don't tell me what to do!" she snapped.

"Put it down, Cyn!" he demanded. "You wouldn't understand what's going on with me."

She crossed her arms. "Then please help me to understand what you're thinking and feeling."

Alex sat down on the bed. "How can you understand the pain I felt when I stepped on that land mine? How can you understand what it feels like to lose a limb fighting overseas in a senseless war when you and every troop serving their country shouldn't be there in the first time?"

"I don't know what it felt like when you were caught in that explosion. And you're right, you shouldn't have been there in the first place, but it's not the end of the world."

"Is that so? You can't understand what it feels like to know that you'll never be able to run again? Or to not be able to swim again in public because people will stare at you and think you're some kind of crippled freak!"

"You're not a crippled freak, Alex," Cynthia replied, placing the prosthetic leg on her husband's left. She sat down and held his hand. "You're still the man I love."

Alex stared at his reflection in the dresser's mirror. "No, I'm not. I'll never be the same again. No matter how hard I pray for the nightmares to end, they keep occurring. I'm constantly imagining pain in my leg and it's no longer there."

"We can get through this, honey," she said, squeezing his forearm.

He removed his hand and looked at his wife. "Please, Cyn, I don't need your pity." He reattached the device and left the bedroom, slamming the door behind him.

Staring at the floor, Cynthia twisted a strand of her micro braid with her index finger while the burning tears ran down her cold cheeks.

≈ ≈ ≈ ≈ ≈

Alex woke up on the living room sofa to the birds chirping in the tree outside on the front lawn. It had been a long time since he heard birds singing so peacefully at this time of the morning. He smiled thinking about the Saturday mornings he spent running along Kelly Drive when the weather broke from the winter. Whatever problems that were on his mind—financial, personal, career, family, etc.—would soon disappear after an intensive, rejuvenating long distance run across the Schuylkill

River testing his physical stamina. Afterwards, he felt exhilarated and tranquil while taking in the moment of his surroundings like the sunlight reflecting off the water; the smell of the green grass; and the birds singing and flying through the sky.

"Those were the days," Alex said, rubbing his amputated leg. His flesh felt cold and rigid. Tilting his head to the right, he checked the time on the entertainment unit. 8:29 AM. He couldn't believe almost six hours passed since his argument with Cynthia. That was the first intense fight they had since he returned home from the hospital. For the past few weeks, Cynthia did her best to accommodate and being careful not to upset him as if she walked on eggshells. A wave of relief overcame Alex after expressing his thoughts and frustrations for the first time. He knew from his counseling sessions with the military psychologist that someday he and Cynthia would have to address the loss of his limb and its subsequent effect on their relationship. Instead, he placed it in the back of his mind and became too wrapped up in his own depression to notice or care until last night.

Alex turned his head towards the stairs when he heard Cynthia open the bedroom door, walk across the wooden floor, and close the bathroom door. Shutting his eyes, he imagined what she was thinking or feeling right about now. Anger. Pain. Isolation. Frustration. Rejection. No, Alex couldn't read her mind, but those were the thoughts and feeling consuming his soul along with guilt. That was the main emotion tearing him apart right now. Resting his forehead in his palms, he thought about all of his attempts to push Cynthia away with his silent, heartless attitude.

"How could I be so stupid?" he mumbled.

Reaching for his artificial limb, Alex assembled the apparatus, climbed the staircase and paused in front of the bathroom. He heard Cynthia turn off the faucets and draw the curtain. Taking two steps forward, he raised his hand to knock on the door. He wanted to apologize for his behavior these past weeks and to make everything up to her, but he didn't. Exhaling a deep sigh, Alex slowly proceeded to walk towards the bedroom until he stopped in his tracks when Cynthia emerged from the bathroom. Turning around, he stared at her with his mouth agape. She looked so beautiful with the lime green bath towel wrapped around her torso. He could smell the sweet fragrance from the shea cocoa butter soap on her radiant skin she used to bathe her body.

Cynthia pursed her lips and stared at Alex's face. She didn't know how to comprehend his facial expression. She barely slept after their argument left her upset, scared and exhausted. She needed to get outside before he woke up to have a moment for her to think and sort her feelings. This morning's shower gave her temporary comfort, allowing the soothing, hot water to massage the tension in her body. She didn't expect to find Alex standing there waiting for her. Cynthia wanted to speak, but decided not to. If her husband maintained his uncooperative stance, what difference would it make at this point?

"Hey," Alex said.

"Hey," Cynthia returned.

"Um, how are you feeling?"

She raised her eyebrows. "Fine."

"Oh, that's good."

"And you?"

He shrugged his shoulders. "Okay, I guess."

Cynthia nodded. "Sleep well?"

Alex shook his head.

She nodded.

"Cyn, I, um, need to, um, can we talk about—"

"About?" she interrupted, crossing her arms.

"Last night," he whispered.

Cynthia sucked her teeth. "I don't know what else is there to say."

"I know I haven't been easy to get along with since coming home and I want to apologize for the way I've been acting," he said, outstretching his arms.

Cynthia pressed her index fingers against her lips. Inhaling deeply, she asked, "So, what brought about this sudden change?"

Alex shared his thoughts and feelings with her from this morning's epiphany. She stood there in the hallway digesting his words while processing their entire relationship since his deployment. Feeling cold, she interrupted by telling him there was something she wanted to share. He nodded as they walked into the bedroom.

"Where did I put it?" Cynthia asked. She snapped her fingers and opened her closet. Pulling out a plastic container, she shifted through the miscellaneous supply of papers until she found what she was looking for: a thick tan journal with the word notes printed in red ink.

Alex rubbed his chin. "What's that?"

"I kept this while you were away," she answered, handing him the journal. "Believe me, honey, you weren't the only one who was suffering."

Alex sat down on the bed and opened the cover. He perused through the contents—Cynthia's thoughts, journal entries, scriptures, e-mail and text message printouts from him, and prayer letters to God—and was amazed that she created and kept this diary. He was so absorbed in the moment that he hardly noticed her getting dressed until she left the bedroom and went downstairs.

Cynthia sat at the kitchen table sipping her coffee. She wasn't in the mood to drink anything, but forced herself to have one cup to shake off the cobwebs from her restless sleep. Her mind was preoccupied with Alex's testimony and her personal feelings. Things weren't easy for either of them these past few weeks, but there was no question she still loved him for better or worse. She turned her head towards her husband when he joined her in the kitchen and sat down beside her.

Alex placed her journal on the table. "Can I ask you a question?"

She nodded and took another sip.

"How come you didn't share this with me sooner?"

"I had a lot on my mind when you came back," she retorted, shrugging her shoulders. "I was so concerned about you and, um, I wasn't ready to. Well, not yet, anyway, but I was planning to. In the beginning, it was rough. I must have sat on the sofa for weeks waiting for you to come walking through the doors after one of your races."

"Where did you get the idea to start this?"

"From a suggestion at the support group meeting your platoon had for all the military wives and girlfriends. At first, I thought it was a dumb idea, but I needed to do something. It helped me get through the loneliness and strengthened my faith while you were gone."

Alex tapped the cover. "Wow. I don't know what to say, Cyn."

She squeezed his hand. "You don't have to say anything. All that matters is you're home with me."

"Well, not all in one piece."

"But you're here with me," she said, kissing his hand.

Closing his eyes, he sucked his teeth and asked, "Do you have any plans for today?"

Cynthia shook her head.

"Um, sometime this afternoon, would you mind taking me to Kelly Drive?"

"Sure, I'd love to."

"I'd like to share something with you, if you don't mind?" Alex clasped his hands and sighed.

"Is everything okay?"

He nodded. "Just thinking this will be the first time I've been there since the accident."

Cynthia pressed her lips. "Oh, honey. I'm so sorry."

He raised his eyebrows. "What for?"

"I know how much you use to love running over there and now you won't be able to. I'm sorry, I didn't mean to—"

"It's okay," Alex interrupted. "I understand what you were trying to say."

"You do?"

He nodded. "Besides, there will be other races."

She raised her eyebrows. "Really?"

He smiled. "Yeah. Like you said, it's not the end of the world."

Cynthia smiled. "No, it's not."

A Test of Faith
Lorraine Elzia

G od has a way of slapping his rebellious children upside the head every now and then and demanding the respect that He deserves. Too often, we are full of ourselves, thinking we are untouchable even by the hands of God. We assume that we are doing our part spiritually by attending church on Sundays and saying a few properly placed Amens at the end of other people's recognition of His worth. Somehow, we think those small gestures of respect for God will be enough to put a cloak of protection over us and shield us from all evil. We feel that because we speak of His existence in our daily banter with others, we have done our part to spread His word. If others ask, "How are you today?" we answer, "Too blessed to be stressed," we feel that we've honored God. We've done our part because others know that we love God and are holy rollers, so to speak, because we are not ashamed to mention God in our everyday conversations. But is that enough? As humans, our answer is "Yes," but would that be the answer of God?

There is a difference between respect and faith. Anyone that believes in God has respect for Him, but not all that do so have faith in Him. God is much more appreciative of the latter. Sometimes, God expects more than mere respect. For some, He says, "Thank you my child for acknowledging that I am the All Mighty. Thank you for understanding that I am Omnipresent and Omnipotent. Thank you for seeing the miracles I have performed and the sacrifices I have made for you, but that is not enough. You are capable of more. I designed you that way, so I expect more from you. *To whom much is given, much is required (Luke 12:48)."*

God demands a little something "extra" from some of us. And sometimes nothing short of His rocking our world will jump start us into accomplishing that something extra that He expects; making us have the spirit to give Him the acknowledgement in the manner that He deserves. Sometimes He takes us to the bottom of the valley in order for us to understand that we have to testify to His glory from the mountaintop. Sometimes He takes his children to the brink of disaster in order for them to understand that they need to be thankful for all that they experience, because their existence, but for His grace, does not have to be. Just like little children, our Father sometimes removes a favorite toy in order for us to be thankful for possessing it. We become shallow and have a mind frame of birthright instead of thankfulness.

Two years ago, I went to a regular doctor's visit. I thought I was doing my part by giving this well-oiled machine of mine an annual tune-up as recommended. Cars require an oil change every 3,000 miles, but that same check up in humans should be done once a year. I always took great pride in doing what was right, and my health was no exception. Feeling fine, and just going through the motions, I walked into my doctor's office without a care in the world, thinking that I would be out in record time with a clean bill of health. I was thirty-eight years old, height and weight proportionate, and although a social smoker and drinker, neither was done in excess. I did not question my health. It never had been a problem in the past, so why would this checkup be any different from the others?

Low and behold, this checkup was different. The tables and the script were seriously turned. As I ranted and raved about just being there to do what I was "supposed" to do annually, my doctor listened to my gibberish and jumped in when she could over my "praise me for my efforts talk" to ask how I was feeling.

"Are you tired? Do you have a headache? Tell me how you feel at this very moment," Ms. MD said with an air of concern hovering over her very existence.

"I feel fine. Why do you ask?" I answered with an air of cockiness.

"Your blood pressure is extremely high. The highest I have ever seen and I have been a doctor for a long time," she said with the same look on her face that you see on cheaply made-for-TV movies. "If I cannot lower it in the next couple of minutes, I am going to have to admit you into a hospital because I think you are on the verge of a heart attack or a stroke."

I looked side to side to survey the room to see if someone else had entered, because in my mind, I knew she couldn't possibly be talking to me. Did she not know who I was? Things like that don't happen to people like me. I am invincible. She had obviously mistaken me with someone else. But there was no one else there. Her words were not meant for another. They were directed towards me. There was no one else in the room; just me, her and an ever-present amount of doom and gloom.

For the next hour, she pumped me with pills, turned down the lights, tried to make me relax and performed an EKG to check my heart. My pressure would not lower despite all her efforts. My sentence was pronounced and she admitted me into the hospital, as she had previously warned.

Once admitted, there were more IVs, prodding, probing and to top off all that madness, the hospital's priest came in. I had been inside a few churches in my life and in a couple of church choirs over the years during the "finding" myself phases of my life. I knew from personal experience what reverends and preachers looked like, but I had never seen a real-life priest before, so that experience was new for me. The corners of my mouth were stuck in the open position as I watched him enter my room. There was something about that black shirt with the white line in the collar, which seemed to impart a higher level of spiritual fear in me than normal.

Black preachers seem more personable, I thought.

"Do you believe in God? What's your religion? Who's your pastor? What are your beliefs on the after life? Would you like to confess your sins?" The young priest spoke to me in a rehearsed manner as if he were reading a scripted checklist instead of talking to me personally about my soul.

"Afterlife? Confess my sins?" My eyebrows raised in disbelief of what was happening. Was he serious?

I gazed at the cross above my hospital bed and felt an electric surge. I was thirty-eight years old and being treated like I was eighty and on my last leg. I refused to accept *man's* diagnosis of *my* life. Staring at the cross on the wall, I thought, *God is the writer of my screenplay, not these doctors, and He hasn't told me that we are in the final act just yet.*

"You can leave my room," I said to the priest with a little snap of the neck that black women are known for. "My blood pressure is rising just looking at your face and the worry on it. You, these doctors, and all these nurses can leave me alone. God is not done with me just yet, so I am not going anywhere," I said defiantly.

I am smart enough to let the doctors do what they do, because after all, they are the mechanics of our bodies, and we all need a good mechanic every now and then. But I also have enough faith in God to trust Him and His will for my life. My trust is in He who has performed miracles and not in man simply because he has an alphabet behind his name.

At the time, I would have considered myself to be religious, but I still had one foot firmly planted in the world. I was at a point in my life that others could tell I believed in God, but I still strayed from seeming preachy or bible toting. I believed in God, I prayed and I spoke of His goodness on command. Yet, I still seemed to have more faith in myself to make things happen. God definitely had a place in my heart, but his position had never been tested there.

That night, confined to a hospital bed, I cried. The weight of the world was upon my shoulders and the realization of my own mortality loomed over my head. I was alone with only my thoughts for companionship. I humbled myself and decided to have a talk with God.

"Lord, although I am not your best servant, I am a good one nonetheless. Why has this happened to me? My finances are in disarray, I hate my house, and I am not where I know I am supposed to be in life and now this? Why, God? Why? I know there are those that suffer far worse than I do, I recognize that and I am thankful for not being in their shoes, but in the scheme of my life, why has this happened? Have you left me, God? Are you trying to teach me a lesson? Have I failed you? What is Your direction for my life?"

And then He spoke directly to me. There was no bright light, parting of clouds or thunderous noise, but His words were crystal clear nonetheless.

"In two years, you will have no worries."

What does that mean? I thought. *Can't He give me more assurance than that?* I marinated on what I was supposed to do with those words. And then it came to me. Pray. Ask for what you want and be confident that He will deliver. Pray that He guides you in the direction you should go and your Father will give you the desires of your heart.

I heard him speak to me again. *"In two years, you will have no worries."*

Those words echoed in my ears over and over again as if someone were yodeling them from a mountaintop. That was all He said to me, and it was Morse code to my ears. Did that mean I would be dead in two years and thus have nothing to worry about? Or did it mean that He was working on my "issues" and they would all be taken care of in two years time? That question was yet to be answered, and it left me feeling perplexed. I thought, *Can You please break it down for me just a little bit, God?*

But I had faith, if only the size of a mustard seed. I evaluated my walk with God. I took a long, hard look at what my relationship had been with Him over the years. As I recalled the memories of hardship in my life and their outcome repeatedly in my mind, I recognized I was hitting the rewind button often. On second glance, I saw that in most of the despairing instances in my life, I talked the talk, but not actually walked the walk concerning God. When the rubber truly met the road, I was not really relying solely on God for deliverance. In the past, when loved one's died, I cried. If I really believed in God as I professed, then there would be no need for tears. That loved one would truly be in a better place; they would be sitting at the feet of the Father unaffected by illness or despair. So, why would there be a need to cry? I should be rejoicing that one of God's angels returned to their place on high. When financial problems arose, instead of giving it over and asking God to fix the problem and teach me not to make the same mistakes again, I put Band-Aids on financial gapping wounds only to see those same financial problems bleed through the bandages because I had not fixed the problems. When my family and friends forsook me, instead of asking God to give me a forgiving spirit, one that recognized that all people sin and fall short at times, I instilled a spirit of resentment and erased them from my life.

I was falling into the same routine and pattern that I had done in the past when my health and the question of my mortality was before me. I looked to myself for the answers instead of raising my head and my hands upward and giving it all over to God. I pushed away one of God's angels, the priest in the hospital, and began my old routine of thinking that I did not need his prayers or the prayers of others because I alone could fix my problem.

I saw just how hypocritical I had been over the years concerning God. I acknowledged Him, but I never put my entire faith in Him. I always put my Faith in myself, and while we need to believe in ourselves because God blesses the child that has his own, we also need to believe in God with all my heart, because all things that are good come from the Lord *(Moroni7: 12)*. We hear sermons in church about how those in the cushy pew seats under the roof of a recognized holy structure can be the most hypocritical people on the face of the earth. We all nod in affirmation at what we hear saying we know others who are like that, but we never think the preacher is actually talking about us. At the crucial moment of my own existence, I remembered the saying, "When you point a finger at someone else, remember that there are four fingers pointing back at you."

I opened my eyes, removed the rose-colored glasses concerning my relationship with God, and truly saw that I was one of those people the pastor was talking about. I reminisced that when others had deaths in their family, financial burdens, spouses or loved ones who had become victim to drugs, crime, etc., I gave them inspirational words, Bible verses and my prayers, all of these thoughts and sentiments were delivered sincerely. I told them, "God's Will be done," and followed it up with urgent instructions that they pray to God and have faith that He would deliver. But those same words seemed to be a hard pill for me to swallow when applying that same rationale to my own life. When those same demons attacked me, I fell victim to worry and doubt. I doubted God and His abilities, and instead, looked to myself and my own capabilities to solve the problems attacking me. Yes, I prayed, but I would surround that prayer with worry while trying to come up with solutions on my own. I relied on Me, instead of relying on God.

In the form of heart failure, God was instructing me to not rely on man, or myself, but to rely on Him.

"If you are going to worry, don't pray, and if you pray, don't worry." Mixing the two does not glorify God. That was His message to me.

I prayed to God without worry of the outcome, something I hadn't done before. I turned it all over to Him, fully expecting and knowing that He would direct my footsteps along whatever path He had for me. During the two years that passed from my scare of death, God guided my footsteps. He turned my world upside down. My family and I went through hell and back. Everyday I prayed for His guidance, steadfast that He would deliver, and everyday He was my tour guide. Things did not go as I planned. Times were tough, but I repeated His words to me constantly in my mind and I had faith that He would come through as He promised. My life took on a new and changed direction. Although it did not change in the manner I would have liked, it changed for the good. My finance problems were alleviated, my burdens were lifted and my health improved after being at the threshold of death's door. The house that I hated was replaced with one I never would have envisioned myself having in this lifetime of mine. All my prayers were answered in grand fashion. It was as if God took an eraser to the chalkboard of my life. The problems of my life were wiped away one by one, leaving behind only dust and particles of past troubles as a memory. In spite of me, God was true to his word in the timeframe He set for me.

As individuals, we want to put God on our schedule. We have expectations and itineraries that we want God to adhere to and show up for in full uniform, dressed in heavenly wardrobe with all the bells and whistles that we expect. We make plans, set goals and then we throw a haphazard prayer His way every now and then while penciling Him in to show up at our upcoming event as guest speaker. We never fully acknowledge that He is the star of the hour and things should go according to His will and His plan. We take his presence for granted. We know that He is part of our lives so we just automatically assume that He will be a part of everything we do. And to some extent, that is true. God is a part of everything we do. but we can't take his appearance in our lives for granted. We want him to move according to our wishes and our demands with the stipulation that He works His miracles in a manner that is pleasing and acceptable in our eyes. "Give me my blessing, Lord! Do it in this manner and do it right now!" That is often the way that we talk to God. However, He hits us over our heads and knocks us down to realize that the best blessings in our lives come when we sit still at His feet, listen to His promises, and have faith that He will deliver.

You have not, because you ask not (James 4:2). Those are magical and miraculous words, to those that will adhere to them. Words and promises that do not fail those who believe. All we have to do is pray, have faith, and believe. If we ask God for the desires of our heart, having faith and believing in Him that he will deliver, and He will do just that. We just need the faith of a mustard seed and remember to remove self from the equation. It is hard for us to not place the burden on ourselves. It is hard for us not to seek results and resolution by our own hands. But the reality is that we are nothing without God. We are nothing without His grace. We need to recognize that our lives will blossom and flourish when we let go of worldly expectations. He was here long before creating us, and He will be here long after we perish. If we want to experience some of His mercy and grace, all we have to do is put our faith in Him. When we do that, He will show up and show out! He may not come when we want or demand Him to, but he is always right on time.

A STROKE OF PURPOSE
Keshia Dawn

The cold rain was full and falling as patches onto the ground. Leslie turned on the car's ignition and waited until the car heated up. Resting her hands in her warm lap, she contemplated returning the phone call she had been putting off. She hesitantly picked up the phone and dialed.

"Hello."

"Hey, Mom. It's me, Leslie."

As though she were blowing the smoke right through the telephone, Alice let her only child know that she was still in her right mind.

"Just because you don't come around or call, I know who you are, chile! What's wrong with your thinking? Never mind. Well," she muttered after taking a long puff on her diminishing cigarette, "Your daddy is in jail. He was acting out again and…"

"Okay." Leslie's breakthrough interruption allowed her a breath while she knew what was coming next.

"Okay? You gonna get him out?"

"Uh, why should I be the one to get him out?"

"Because he's your father, Leslie! Because he's the same man that kept a roof over your head for eighteen years. That's

49

why. What's wrong with you? You just too good, huh? You in the corporate world and your heart is as cold as them, huh?"

"No, it's not that at all. I mean, you're his wife. Look, I was your child, isn't that what parents are suppose to do, provide a roof over their child's head?" Frustrated without even getting an answer, Leslie concluded, "Look I'm on my way into work and it's raining. I really need to watch where I'm going. Goodbye."

Since the age of five, Leslie could remember her parents raising her on their problems. Leslie endured all the painful memories: the blackened eyes that graced her mother's face; the stab wounds that her father owned due to Alice's defense mode; her many bloody noses due to the nervousness from the arguments that woke her up out of her sleep; or her lack of appetite to eat because of an upset stomach. For years, she tried to talk her parents into understanding what they were doing to her, but, they wouldn't listen. Now, her mother labeled her *too good* for the family, yet unable to see the hurt in her only child.

Leslie slowly backed her vehicle out of her driveway. Feeling the onset of a stress headache, thanks to her conversation with her mother, Leslie slammed on the brakes immediately. She rambled through her purse and searched for her blood pressure medication. Pain immediately shot up her arm, across her shoulders and down her backside. Thinking it was just a muscle spasm, Leslie rubbed every inch of her being, trying to smooth out the kinks, but the intensity was greater than she expected. Her colorful world became black and white, distant, and then, gone.

A Stroke of Purpose

≈ ≈ ≈ ≈ ≈

"Leslie. Leslie. It's Derrick, honey. Can you hear me?"

Hearing her husband's voice made Leslie want to open her eyes, but it wasn't happening no matter how hard she tried. She tried to open her mouth and respond to his question, but she couldn't get her lips to part. Something just wasn't right.

Derrick! I hear you, but I can't open my mouth! What's wrong with me? Derrick, I feel your hand, but I can't squeeze back to let you know that I'm okay. I'm okay...I think!

Something was definitely wrong, but it would take more to help her realize exactly what it was. Her only recollection was that she was sitting in her car and the fierce headache that crept into her being. Leslie remembered not being able to get to her medication in time.

"Doctor Thornton! Please let me know what's going on with my wife!" A distressed Derrick rushed the doctor before he had his feet settled into the ICU room.

Walking toward the bed where Leslie's twisted body lay, Dr. Thornton lifted his young patient's chart.

"Mr. Bryant—"

"Call me Derrick, please," he requested while standing his six feet tall rugged self near the doctor.

"Mr. Bry... uh, Derrick, your wife has suffered an ischemic attack. A stroke as you would know it. Thankfully, your neighbor found her in a significant amount of time. Her oxygen levels are slightly fair. She's battling ...." the doctor shared while looking directly into the young man's face.

"Oh no!"

Derrick hung his head low and examined his wife's body "Can she recover? Will she? Will she remain in this form?" He covered his trembling mouth with his hand as tears trailed down his face.

This form? Oh, God, what has happened to me?

"Right now, nothing can be said for anything. Leslie can go in any direction, but we are praying for the best. She's in a coma, and you know, it's going to be up to Leslie to pull through."

Allowing the tears to stream from the dam of his ducts, Derrick could only think of one thing. "Praying," he said. "Does the hospital have a chapel? I need to go...now!" He almost begged while clasping his hands together behind his head.

Dr. Thornton lead Derrick out of the hospital room and toward the hospital's chapel, planning to stay and pray with the young husband as he sent prayers on him and his wife's behalf.

Don't go! Don't leave! was all a comatose, spirited Leslie could try and yell out. Taking into everything she overheard, Leslie searched for comfort in her comatose state. Her mind was filled with life as she knew it. How it was and how it was supposed to be were now her only thoughts.

Lord, I'm tired. All I've ever wanted was to be loved by my parents and this is what I get? All I've ever wanted was to have someone in my corner. Since I was a little girl, I've only had me. Where were You? Why didn't you rescue me? Why didn't you send someone to take me away from the hurt and pain?

Leslie quieted her voice and granted her wish toward heaven, waiting on her answer. *Take me, I'm ready. It just doesn't matter anymore.* She waited and listened for what was next to come. She heard someone coming into the hospital room.

"I told you, Les, I told you not to worry. You have to let it go. That's what I kept telling you! You can't take on your parents' burdens anymore. I need you here with me Les…we're not through!"

Although they had been married for ten years, Derrick had been in her life for the past twenty years. He knew all about the trials and tribulations that weighed heavy on Leslie's heart. He saved her so many times from losing her mind when she thought she'd have no choice in the matter.

Derrick, I know. I know. I thought I had put it all behind me, but when we found out we couldn't have kids I felt cheated! I felt my life was not fair. Why should I have to suffer my whole childhood just to find out that I can't have babies of my own? I could have done it, Derrick! I could have loved those children the way that I longed for. I could have shown them how it feels to be loved by a mother who puts her kids first before a man that beats me, mistreats me and the kids. Don't you hear me, Derrick? I'm hurting.

A loud commotion was heard coming down the hall. Derrick, releasing his wife's motionless hand, hurried to the door. Wiping his eyes with the back of his hand, Derrick caught sight of his mother-in-law at the nurse's station wearing a sweater over her gown.

"Mrs. Alice!"

Turning in a quick motion, Alice didn't give the nurse enough time to finish her statement once she caught sight of her son-in-law. With her arms above her head and pointing in his direction, Alice vented her anger toward Derrick.

"How dare you! You don't have no right! You have no right to keep this away from me!"

"What are you talking about?" Confused with the arguing stature of Alice, Derrick went in defense mode. "I have every right, too, Mrs. Alice, every right. I am her husband." Derrick blocked the hospital door and stood stern. "You will not, and I mean will not go into this room with your loud screaming and yelling! Mrs. Alice, I've always respected you, but I will no longer allow you and your husband to hurt Leslie anymore!"

Feeling shame come over her at first, Alice's anger stepped in. "Hurt Leslie? Hurt Leslie. Be for real!" She calmed down and looked past him. "Leslie hurts me. She doesn't even come to visit or call. You want to talk about hurt. Honey, let's talk about it!"

"Do you know why? Because she's been needing you and wanting you as a mother for her whole life!"

Standing eye to eye with her daughter's husband, Alice stood frozen from the comment. Looking backward to see if the nurse's were paying attention, Alice didn't shift. "Move!" she commanded, pushing Derrick aside and making her way into the room. Looking over her shoulder as she made her way around the curtain, Alice fell to her knees when she saw Leslie.

"Oh my God! Oh, no!"

Derrick, who is it?

"Leslie, baby! What have I done? What's wrong with my baby, Derrick? What's wrong?" She asked, looking up at her son-in-law's face. "What's going on?"

Crying as if she hadn't lived her life the way she had by choosing herself and her ignorant abusive husband over her daughter, the mother figure that Leslie longed for became coherent.

Dropping his hands to meet Alice's hands, he pulled her up to her feet.

"I know, Alice. It was a stroke. The doctor said her stats are steady, but there is no way for us to know either way. She's in a coma."

Alice frowned, closed her eyes and asked, "Is she in pain, Derrick? Is her body hurting?"

"They have her on medication. I don't think she's in pain."

After moaning and rocking in Derrick's arms for as long as she could stand it, Alice walked over to her daughter's body. Leaning in to kiss Leslie's twisted mouth, Alice dropped her face to lie beside her daughter's cold and unrecognizable face.

I don't want her here! Leslie screamed. *I don't want her here Derrick! She hurt me.*

"I'm, I'm sorry. I'm sorry, Leslie. I'm sorry, sorry, sorry! Please don't leave me before I let you know that I didn't mean it! I know you probably don't want me here. But...I can't go."

You heard that? Leslie questioned the air.

55

Derrick made eye contact with Alice and eased his crumbled spirit and body out of the somber room. Giving the fifty-eight-year-old mother time alone with her daughter was what was needed in case she didn't get the chance again.

Alice took a seat close to Leslie's bed, leaned in and took her daughter's contracted hand.

"I hurt you," she started with a soft, whimpering voice. "And the stupid thing about it, I know I did. Over and over. I took the role of motherhood and didn't protect it. I abused it.

But I was hurting even before the age of ten, Mama!

"I heard you when you were five and your eyes full of fear and tears, asking me to leave your daddy. And when you were nine and wanted to move from me. I was scared, no, I was jealous because you were stronger than me then. You had courage to want to leave and I had only played with the thought."

Listening to her mother's words, Leslie took a chance to ask another question just to see if her mother had really heard her. If God had intervened and allowed their spirits to talk, Leslie wanted to fulfill her heart's desire. She needed the pain to go!

I was strong because of you. You gave me the idea. You left, but went back. I needed you to stay away from him! That's all I wanted!

Only hearing with her heart, Alice answered her daughter. "Baby, I know what you wanted. I tried leaving and coming back, but he was your father. I didn't want you to be angry with me for raising you without him in your life. I didn't want you to hate me, but I guess you wound up hating me anyway!"

I don't hate you. I hurt for you! I know he was my father, but I was a child that needed peace. He brought pain and it's still here! Oh, God, if you're allowing my mom to hear me, thank You. Thank You! Mommy, I don't hate you. I've just needed you to be there for me!

"I guess it just all turned for the worse once you got older. You didn't seem as if you needed me. And then your teacher, Mrs. Fritz, came into your life, helped you with school, then college. I wanted to be apart of that, but by that time, I had let you down. I was too old and who would want me? Where would I go?

"I'm so proud of you! You went to college and did it on your own. I was jealous of that, but now I see I was wrong to be. You saw no change in me because I didn't. I didn't change. I allowed your daddy to fight me, again and again. And I let you see all of that!" Alice didn't notice Derrick walking back into the room until she felt his hands on her shoulders. "And the situation never changed. It went from physical abuse but the verbal abuse stayed! I'm sorry. What did I do? Oh God, what did I do to my baby?"

"Mrs. Alice, Mrs. Alice. It's okay. Leslie knew you wanted to, but didn't have the strength. Didn't have the courage. She just wanted you to at least say something."

"No! That's all an excuse and it's not okay! I made up excuses. I was to into me to help my baby through college, to help her move into her very first apartment. I was selfish and now my baby is going to leave me!" Alice wallowed in her guilt for leading her daughter down the path of years of depression.

No! No! God no! Please don't do this. I want to stay! I want to stay with my mom! She does love me. She knows what she did, please bring me back!

Resting her head on Leslie's hospital bed, Alice's cried as she prayed to God.

"Lord, I know You hear me because You have allowed my daughter to grow into this beautiful woman that I prayed that she would be. You allowed her to be stronger than me and run from men that were like her dad. I know You hear me because I've asked You to allow me to have the conversation she's always wanted to have. Please don't let this be too late. Please, God, don't let this be too late!"

Not wanting his mother-in-law to ill herself, Derrick gathered Alice and walked her unwillingly out of the hospital room. Taking the plastic cup of water from the nurse on duty, he led Alice to a set of open seats just down the hall. Sitting next to her limp body, Derrick handed the water to Alice and made sure she drank enough to soothe her.

"Thank you."

"Oh, the nurse brought this to you, I guess she—"

"I mean thank you," she interjected, sipping another gulp of water, "for taking care of Leslie. I knew when I met you that you'd take care of her. My baby." She concluded, looking over at Derrick.

Derrick responded. "You don't have to thank me for that. She's my wife. I've loved her even before."

Sitting silent for the remainder of the minutes that had passed, the monotony ended when Derrick went over to the nurses and asked questions about his wife's long-term condition.

దు దు దు దు దు

The days turned into plenty, the weeks passing holidays and the holidays nearing the New Year. In between life continuing as usual, Leslie found her way into the temple that God had created just for her. Life as she knew it wouldn't be the same. It wasn't because of the slight limp that she now walked with or the slur in her face whenever Derrick made her laugh. It couldn't even be because of the physical therapy that kept her busy most of her long days. Life would be different because of the relationship God had formed just for her.

On the day she was blessed to open her eyes again, her mother was right there. Although she couldn't yet speak, she told Alice that she forgave her with her eyes. A month later when her voice returned, Leslie cried in her mother's arms and let her know that she heard everything. "I love you, too," were the first words she spoken gracefully toward her mother.

Shocked, while rubbing Leslie's hair in a back motion, Alice, smoke free and husbandless, smiled at Leslie. "My baby. Oh, honey, you're talking! I love you, too!" Kneeling down, Alice kissed her daughter.

Nothing needed to be reiterated for actions showed louder than words. Just looking at her mother who became her full time caregiver, age took off of her whole being. Life wasn't all good for her because of her own actions, but with God's grace and mercy, He allowed Alice a second chance.

Alice never made it to the jail house to retrieve her self-righteous husband as she had in all the other years. She stayed put, never leaving for more than an hour at a time just to change clothes. One day without thinking even further on her thoughts, Alice asked Derrick to accompany her and he did so.

Two hours was all it took for her to pack all the essentials that she would ever need. Leaving furniture and taking only her personal belongings, Alice gathered memorabilia for herself and Leslie and left. Having the talk that Derrick sparked, Alice happily accepted her role as full time caregiver for her daughter and would indeed move in with them.

"I left for me," Alice said, driving Leslie from her physical therapy appointment.

"I know," Leslie responded.

"But," she paused, turning to look at her daughter while the car sat at a stop sign, "you gave me the strength and the courage to do it. I did it for me so that I could be some good for you. I owe you and don't tell me I don't." She held her hand to halt a responsive Leslie. She looked both ways before going forward. "I owe you the rest of me."

"You know I appreciate that and you know that's all I've ever wanted, Mommy! But God is good. There is still time for you to have a life of your own. I wouldn't feel right if—"

"Girl, you know Alice gone live! Now you *know* Alice gonna live!" Alice jerked her head toward her daughter and then back to the road. "Matter of fact my fortieth class reunion is coming up, how 'bout we go do the girl thing and shop?"

"I'm game!"

"And you should be. You're going to be my date so you may as well get ready, chile!"

"I'm ready!" Leslie joked with her mother as she pointed and smoothed the wrinkles out of her nylon jogging suit.

Alice wiped a tear from her eye "I'm ready. I'm ready too, honey."

THE VANILLA ROOM
Agnes B. Levine

I was so afraid, so angy. I was alone in the Vanilla Room. The ugly, brown-speckled ceramic tiles all around my bare, toffee-colored feet and red-polished toenails scared me. It was dizzying for me to look at the many splatters of specks on the cream-colored blocks. They were all over the place just like my rapid thoughts. The blocks resembled the gridlocks of my life blurred by the burning tears I refused to let fall.

I looked around and saw nobody there. It was just me, four vanilla walls, a colorless door with a small opaque window, one black mat, and those seemingly endless, ugly brown-speckled tiles. A vanilla room.

I was going to hold onto my will and stay in control of my tears, though my mind was already leaving me. I had enough of my life as I was living it. That was how I got there. "Damnit!" I yelled, kicking the black mat across the speckled tiles with such force. It slammed against the far wall and slid up before crashing down with a loud flap. "Open the door!" My hip hurt from the might of the kick. The tiles blinked a cautious yellow and laughed at me. That was not enough to free myself and leave this place. My anger and frustration intensified as tears fell. The more I cried, the more I screamed, yelled and hollered. My thoughts moved even faster and I begged them to slow down. "Please, please!" I pleaded at the top of my lungs. The more I tried to keep up with them, it hurt like a horrible migraine headache. Defeat was killing me.

I always had that good ole determination to have it my way or no way. My way was to single-handedly change my world. The Vanilla Room was how that ideal of mine came crashing down with such power, I was incapacitated. The exact words the doctors used were *nervous breakdown*. To them and the world, I was a crazy, blabbering, blubbering fool. To me, I was angrily responding to each and every pervasive, racing thought. There were millions of them, bottled-up from years and days gone by. Frustrations and pains I kept to myself. There were too many to contain in my head any longer. I spoke those thoughts to give them release from my mind. Speaking. Responding. My thoughts overpowered me. In time, it was futile trying to respond to each one. Once my mind, my spirit, and my soul could not take it any longer, they split up and sent my body screeching to a halt that fateful morning in 1993. Slowly, but deliberately, the resilient walls I erected came tumbling down until I was whisked off to a hospital and locked inside the Vanilla Room.

I screamed, hollered, cursed and cried as I was consumed with anger and frustration. All the while, my mind, now freed, zipped around the room, darting around and in between the brown-speckled tiles. I was crazy. The demons, or negative thoughts, that overwhelmed my mind, then threatened to arrest what was left of my weary soul. The dingy yellow specks blinked faster than I could keep up with. A vengeful plot of countless exhausting realities of working two jobs; a stressful marriage to a drug-addicted husband; being a struggling night school student while mothering three children, including a severely developmentally-delayed child; being a daughter, sister, friend, juggling bills; and living in poverty forced my mind to perceive those blinking speckled tiles as a warning. Death! Death! Death a-coming!

I was doing the normal parent things such as checking homework, feeding and clothing the family, providing school lunch money, settling sibling disputes, and shuffling the kids to their recreation activities. With my developmentally-delayed son, there were extraordinary responsibilities: making sure his special supplies and medications were well-stocked and in his book bag for school and communicating with his case worker, specialty clinics, teacher, school nurse, physicians or, later, private-duty nurses daily. I woke up extra early in the mornings to administer his medications and start his breakfast, which required special care since he could not eat by mouth, walk or talk. I was hopelessly and co-dependently trapped inside *superwoman* who was stuck on the floor of the Vanilla Room. Fear escalated in a split second, and then, I felt like I exploded.

I fell, kneeling on the black mat with a weighty drop. Now the pain at my knees triggered the tears to pour. I lost control. "Stop!" Stubborn me was no more. I was submissive. I wailed uncontrollably. "Please, just stop me. Help me, God, help me!" I sobbed. The black mat welcomed me even more. I noticed that the thoughts stopped. However, when they did so, my heartbeats replaced their rapid speed, forcing me to fear that my organ would explode inside my chest at any moment.

All of a sudden, I seemed to be in a murky river. My grandmother, who died when I was a child, appeared and visited me in this river. I felt her chubby brown arms cradling me. "Help me, please!" I called to her. I smelled her favorite Blue Magic hair grease under her thin, silver-blue hair. Her hair was perfectly groomed although we were in the water. It was calming. I had absolutely no thoughts, no noticeable heartbeat, just peace. Then she vanished. I blinked and I was not in the murky river anymore. I was in a black hole. The number 63 glared at me out of nowhere. As I regained focus, the number gradually transformed into the letters E.R. I was still on the black mat. Eventually, I could clearly see that there were letters on the black mat that I never noticed before. Apparently, the letters indicated the mat belonged in the Emergency Room. However, I later learned that my grandmother's grave marker was Number 63. There was an emergency here and Jesus came.

As I lay on the mat trying to make sense of what I just experienced, I curled into the fetal position and cried softly. "Help me." The tears were the remainder of my emotions flowing. "Help me." I understood the warning that the life I was living would kill me. I needed help out of the life I had created, but had no idea where to turn. "Somebody, please help me." It seemed the world was out to get me with unbelievable strength and the Vanilla Room was its latest weapon. I did not know how and if I would ever leave there. It was my toughest challenge. I squeezed my eyes shut, hoping to magically find remnants of my superwoman personality and exit the room. She was gone. Vanished from me just like my grandmother had seconds, or was it minutes, earlier? The reality that there was no superwoman to conquer all things depressed me. I searched all over my mind for help as my spirit beckoned me to be still, but to no avail. I feared my sane mind had long since left the room, never to return. I was no match for my surroundings.

Soon, the hasty thoughts returned to consume me again. I panicked. I could not take that anymore. "Oh, no!" I tried to scream and move. Realizing I did not even have the energy to straighten out on the mat or respond to the thoughts as I had before, I remembered the one thing my mother always told me to do when I could not do anything else about life's circumstances being out of my control.

"Call on Jesus and believe He will come," she always said.

However, I did not know how to call Him. I did not have the strength to kneel and pray. As badly as I wanted to, the many fast thoughts were too distracting. They picked up speed again. My mind was very sick and it was killing me.

And then I heard a whisper among those thoughts. "Jesus."

In reflex, my spirit responded in kind to the whisper. "Jesus?" I simply whispered.

The various thoughts persisted, but so did the whisper. "Jesus." I continued to concentrate and repeat His name each time I heard it. But I could not control the thoughts and images of my difficult life of living with a drug user in and out of recovery. The badge I had worn so proudly most of my life was slowly being torn from my chest. I made one more futile attempt to regain control.

"Okay, that's enough!" I finally yelled. "Open your eyes and get up off the floor!" The command hit the walls and slid to the floor. "Get up!" I screamed with more determination than before. The response, however, was just the same. The words bounced from the wall to the floor. A door stood staring at me. It's cloudy eye was taunting me. "Get up!" It teased. "See the world that knocked you down!"

With all my strength, I tried to pull myself up and reach the door. Now the door was more stubborn than me. It held its distance from where I lay, my strength never pulling me off the mat. Spirit stared some more at the tiles of my life. Although they were angled differently than before, the scenes were all the same. I couldn't move a muscle other than my heaving chest, heavy heart, crying eyes, and weary soul. They all teamed up to transform stubbornness into an excruciating frustration. Not being able to pull myself together kept my mind separated.

Then I became angrier. I was so angry I was mad. My life was snatched from me without any warning. The rug that weaved my dreams and aspirations, though tattered at the edges, was instantly yanked away, knocking me down shamefully. I felt alone, for my husband had long since toppled over after having succumbed to drugs. My marriage was over again. The same old ugly tiles held my despair for me to see, now closer and in the most vivid detail against the mat. The eviction notices and utility turn-off notices taped to the refrigerator that emptied in between paychecks. The paychecks I labored tirelessly for always shrunk before being deposited into my over-drafted account. Everything was speckled across the tiles and shouting, "Failure! You horrible mother!"

I covered my ears and cried even more. Everything that was wet seemed to rush out of me and my whole body seemed to deflate gradually, allowing the persecuting thoughts to slow to a whisper before total silence engulfed me. No more tears. Nothing, but extreme serenity.

I instantaneously became aware of a force overtaking me. An intense and almighty, invisible presence that cradled me, comforted me, and reassured me that I had not failed. I saw the same images of my life appear and pause in my mind. The feeling of stubbornness was replaced by self-motivation. Self-motivation became self-love. Self-love became euphoria and it grew more and more intense until my whole being was consumed by it.

I understood my circumstances differently than I had before. Superwoman had stolen every opportunity I had had to pause. She distorted my dreams and aspirations, too. I was afraid of what I became. I was afraid of the lifestyle I had created. I was afraid of superwoman and her extraordinary energy. It was not the tangible leaps and bounds I sought, it was peace and happiness. I was trying to achieve this or that to be able to experience peace and happiness in life. Once and for all, I wanted the superwoman in me reduced to woman. I yearned to arrest the compulsive-holic in me. I eagerly wanted to exist in that comfortable, inviting space in between the frames of my life that I discovered, not my death.

My tears became caresses. The warmness streamed lovingly from my eyes and a stirring in my stomach cushioned the fall of my old, burdened spirit. I was also surrendering. I relinquished the last of those mental strongholds over to that Omnipresence in the Vanilla Room that seemed to absorb them so willingly. I surrendered my wants and desires for that perfect life unto the presence I recognized as my Savior, Jesus Christ. I trusted that higher power to save me from superwoman and He did. The more I trusted, the more I felt a tremendous weight lifted from me, and then an elevation of my body. I watched this event take place in such an eerie way. I saw myself hanging on a cross over the black mat. I watched myself levitate toward a light brighter than I could keep mine eyes on. I felt a super-sensational, intense feeling of love that I never wanted to be apart from.

My Spirit unburdened to God how angry I was with my life and its circumstances. No matter how hard I studied in school, I had to always settle for a B. No matter how hard I performed at work, my evaluations were mediocre below an unbreakable, seven years strong, glass ceiling, although my services were in high demand by my employer. How insurance companies controlled my grocery list, and lack of affordable housing controlled the amount of quality time I could spend with my children. How my husband's addiction fueled an emotionally, physically, and mentally abusive marriage. How bureaucracy and discrimination controlled having a special needs child in the home and community. How racism was destroying His kingdom; therefore, it was too easy for the poor and needy to lose faith. I had lost faith. And how justice was just a word and why did

He turn His back on me, the helpless and hopeless modern-day Job? All of this and much more poured out of me in that Vanilla Room. The crazy woman's babbling conversation with God. I had subconsciously taken on all the world's problems—isn't that what a superwoman did?

Remarkably, I began seeing a series of events that I did not understand, including my father's unexpected transition from this earth. These visions culminated with the world exploding into a zillion shattered pieces disappearing into tremendous, blinding brightness, and I heard a voice resounding, "When these things come to pass, you will know it is Me!"

I was levitating towards brightness that was warming me all over, inside and out. I felt the love bursting from my heart and moving down my arms through my fingers and then traveling along my legs. I felt my legs support my weight. I felt an enormous burden lift from my shoulders as I stood crying tears of immense joy. I could feel God's love washing through me. My thoughts were only on God's love filling me. It was very soothing and comforting.

When I opened my eyes, I was still in a euphoric state of mind, but I noticed now that the ceramic tiles in the Vanilla Room were now glistening, gold-speckled ones. I turned around and looked at the walls. They were still vanilla. The door was still there, too, with its small, opaque window, but I knew it was reachable. I looked down at my toffee feet with my nicely polished red toenails. I instantly remembered that polishing my toenails was one of the very few nice things I did for myself. I smiled. I vowed to do them as long as I live. My testament to loving myself. My mind had returned, and though it was a little fast and hazy, it remembered with remarkable detail all that had occurred. My spirit seemed rejuvenated with such joy that it made my heart quicken in delight. I wanted to run, jump, and share what I had experienced with everyone I knew. In fact, I did. "Jesus came! He came! Jesus, my Savior, came and rescued me!" I informed everybody after that experience. My life transformed drastically along with my mind.

It is crucial for my sistahs to understand how very burdened my mind was at that time. In the weeks leading up to the Vanilla Room, I rarely slept. I was very disappointed that my son would not stabilize and that my husband's drug use would not cease. I was even more frustrated and disappointed that I could not control either one just as I had no control of being among those selected to be included in the firm's down-sizing. However, I blamed myself and believed that if I had made different choices in my past, God would never had abandoned me. I remember being extremely depressed several weeks prior to arriving at the hospital. The lost of appetite, loss of sleep, always feeling as if I would cry though no tears would come, feelings of hopelessness meaning I could not imagine one good thing happening to me that would bring me happiness in even the smallest measure, lost of interest in school, family, friends, television, church, etc. I had began to exist like a zombie being void of any feeling or emotion other than anger. Eventually I lost sense of time and nights and days. Every day was dark after awhile and the sun became just an annoyance for me to hide from under covers. Then all my energy drained out of me. It was impossible for me to stand long enough at the sink to wash a fork or brush my teeth. Therefore, I skipped those tasks. Obviously, this meant I fell behind in my hygiene and housework and responsibilities as a parent and I slowly closed myself off from my family. I felt ashamed and tried to even hide from God. I share these details to encourage and inspire others to recognize these symptoms in self and loved ones and then seek treatment immediately.

Because I have also accepted that depression is anger turned inwards, I returned to writing as a coping measure and I also turned to bible study because I had to understand how to love those who hurt you. I had to understand that God does not leave us, we leave Him. Leaving the Vanilla Room was a process of a short stay in the hospital receiving mental health care and coping skills. It also meant eleven medications and the loss of most of the skills I had mastered prior to arriving in the Vanilla Room, including my speech, ability to write, sit, walk, cook, type, read, drive, bathe and do my own hair and nails, go shopping, etc. I had to work very hard to regain all those skills, and that included participating in a mental health rehabilitative day program.

In addition, as I educated myself about mental illnesses such as Bi-Polarity (Manic Depression), which is my diagnosis, I felt less ashamed. I felt less ashamed because I realized I was not alone in living with this illness and that I could live in harmony with the illness to be productive in society. God manifested Himself in my life stronger and stronger bringing me more and more peace and happiness. I shed my fear that people would learn I had a mental illness. I focused on what would God want me to do? I devised a personal wellness plan helping me to take advantage of resources such as therapy, counseling, self-motivation and self-determination, and I made major lifestyle changes and decisions. Some decisions and choices have been more painful than others, such as realizing both my husband and I had incompatible illnesses and accepting the reality that I could not take care of my son at home anymore.

I have accomplished nothing absent of God's presence in my life. Since being in the Vanilla Room, I have completed a Masters in Public Administration Degree, with a Minor in Legal and Ethical Studies. I teach part-time, serve with many volunteer organizations, and have become a full-time writer. I found renewed confidence in abilities and myself as a child of God. I went from taking 11 medications in 1993 to just two today in 2007. I take long walks, swim, and garden. It was a slow, agonizing process recovering, but having surrendered to Him, I exchanged my old lifestyle for a more peaceful, happy one. I live my life with purpose and prepare for eternity with God by holding fast to His will, not mine. I make time to smell the flowers. Though I sometimes stumble, I get back up and stay focused, always nurturing God's blessings.

Some of the meaningful supports that have helped me along the way in addition to family and close friends have been my church families, community groups, Bible study, Nar-Anon, Alcoholics Anonymous (no, I don't drink or use substances, but the twelve steps apply to co-dependency which is just as bad), therapy/counseling, and the National Association on Mental Illness (NAMI).

Some of the visions I had in 1993 have already come to pass which confirms in my spirit that God loves me. One reoccurring vision I had while I was still unable to speak, read, bathe, etc., was me sitting at a computer typing. Ain't God awesome!

DISCOVERING THE JOY WITHIN
Allyson Deese

Oh God, NO! Please don't take my babies!" Jordyn cried as she tried to jump into the six foot pit that stared up at her. Held back by her sobbing father, the young mother stood looking down into the grave of her two beautiful twins. The two tiny caskets were light pink, and the rain was hitting them ever so gently, as if God himself was crying, because they were coming home to Him. But Jordyn, a new mother, didn't see it that way. She wanted them home with her. For home was they place they belonged. Safe and warm in her arms. All she could see were her two beautiful babies being taken away from her. It was just a few days ago that she gave birth, welcoming them into this world. Within an hour, they were both gone. Instead of bringing them home to their awaiting nursery complete with two cribs and a glider, family and friends had gathered to say good-byes to the two that never got a chance to say hi. Her heartfelt tears of pain began anew as she recited a poem to her babies. Painfully, she sobbed the words with gut-wrenching emotion to her angels.

Allyson Deese

Angels

Just as God gave you to me,
He needed you more. His son, Jesus Christ,
Wanted you by his very side.
Grammy, Nannie, and MaVia wanted to
care for you and shower you with all of their
love and affection.
Oh, angels, how I miss you so,
My babies, I never wanted to let you go,
but, GOD, himself, wanted you too.
It's mommy's prayer that we will meet again.
But until I see your beautiful faces, know that
I love you with everything that I am, and everything that
I dream to be.

Jordyn could smell the rain long before the first drop ever fell from the sky. And even though the drops were falling harder and heavier against her shoulders, the heart broken seventeen year old couldn't bear to leave her precious babies' sides. She tried her hardest to hold on to the few moments they shared. She pictured in her mind over and over again just how sweet and innocent they looked as they took their final breaths. Both girls had smiles on their faces, as if they knew that they were going to meet their Jesus. The beautiful angels had quietly and all too quickly slipped away.

In the mist of the treacherous rain, a rainbow appeared, but Jordyn could not see the joy in it. All she could feel was her pain as the raindrops mixed with her tears. Her tears fell as hard as the rain, until she could no longer decipher which was which.

"Why, Momma? Why did He take my little babies away?" Jordyn fell into her mother's arms. She simply didn't understand how a loving God could take away the babies she had carried inside of her for six long months.

"Jordyn, He makes no mistakes. I know it's hard but you've got to accept this and keep your trust in God." Even as Lorraine spoke soothing words to try and comfort her daughter, she too, was shedding tears. All David Thomas, Jordyn's father, could do was wrap his loving arms around his fragile daughter.

All Jordyn wanted was for the pain to go away. Only poor Jordyn did not know just how much pain she would have to endure before she discovered her joy within. Not even the love and support of her parents could ease the loss of her twins. A part of her very soul had been laid to rest.

At home that night Jordyn lay in bed. She was wide-awake because her eyes simply wouldn't close and allow her to give into darkness. Jordyn knew that closing her eyes meant facing the monster she had once loved. In her dreams, she would see Carlos. Then she would have to relive that day over again. The day that changed her life forever. Her eyelids fluttered like butterflies as she fought the sleep that her body so desperately needed.

The Greatest Gift of Love
To give you the greatest gift of love
would mean pure joy for me.

Allyson Deese

I love you,
In spite of how you act.
Unconditionally, I love you.
That's why I want to give you
God's greatest gift of Love.
A baby,
The greatest gift of love.

That's how Jordyn felt the day she found out she was pregnant by Carlos Johnson. But Jordyn had soon learned that not even being pregnant would save her from the abuse of Carlos. She walked on eggshells around him because the last thing she needed was to upset him and have him put his hands on her. As her belly grew bigger, it was harder and harder to protect her babies while trying to avoid his harsh and violent blows.

She never knew what she was saying or doing to set him off. Sometimes he would just look at her and get angry. It's as if he hated or even despised her. He always saw fault in her. But after every beating came more apologies; more claims of love; and too many un-kept promises of 'it won't ever happen again.'

Jordyn hid her bruises from the world. There was makeup to cover black eyes. Just a bit of rouge would disguise bruised cheeks incurred from his hard slaps. Her clothing covered the discoloration left by hard fists and painful kicks to her stomach, back, or wherever the blows landed. She rarely wore short sleeves or shorts. Friends and family couldn't know that she was being abused. Jordyn did not want to be judged and she wanted no one judging Carlos.

He loved her. At least he said that he loved her. Sadly, he didn't know how to control his anger. She was always doing something to provoke him. *Wasn't she?* Well, she didn't know what it was, but she shouldn't have been doing it. A seventeen year old girl should be happy that a twenty year old man would even look at her twice. Right? Especially a seventeen-year-old girl who was bulging, heavy set and wearing a size sixteen.

Yep, she considered herself lucky to have him. But she didn't realize how far from the truth that was until that day. The dreadful day she couldn't keep him away from her stomach. The day she, as a mother, was unable to protect her unborn babies.

As usual, Carlos picked Jordyn up from school that day as he had done every day since they had been dating. She was talking with a group of friends when he pulled up. Trying not to anger him, she said good bye to her friends and hurried to the older model Buick.

"Hey, Baby!" she greeted him while closing the heavy door.

"Don't you 'Hey Baby' me!" She didn't know what she had done wrong but she could tell he was pissed. His eyes were bloodshot red; obvious effects of getting high on marijuana. He often times was high and out of his mind. "How many times I got to tell you not to be 'round other men? How am I suppose to know them my babies you carrying if you always got other men up in your face?"

Carlos was always accusing her of cheating with some man. Jordyn wasn't surprised. It used to flatter her. But that was before she realized his accusations stemmed from his own infidelities. She had never been unfaithful. It was him who was always getting caught up with some other woman. Then, as if she was wrong for finding out, he would beat Jordyn.

"Carlos, we were just talking about homework," she nervously tried to explain.

Jordyn wasn't interested in either of the boys in her group of friends. She had known them both since kindergarten. All they were and ever will be is friends.

Carlos didn't respond. He was mad as hell and she was going to be punished as

soon as he got her home. His mom was at work and they had the house to themselves.

She was going to stop disrespecting him. He knew Jordyn was messing around. She had to be. There was no way the twins could be his.

Jordyn was so nervous as they rode in silence. They past the turn off for her house so she knew he would be taking her to his place. His mother was gone. There would be no one there to protect her from his violence. She wanted to jump out of the car and run, but how could she jump out of a car moving fifty miles per hour in her condition?

The beating started as soon as they walked into the small house. He closed the front door by slamming her body into it.

"Carlos, no!" she screamed as she wrapped her arms around her stomach protectively. Carlos responded with more slaps.

The blows grew more and more intense. She soon fell into a heap on the floor. Jordyn pulled her knees to her stomach and lay in the fetal position. Her back caught most of his punches and kicks.

"Whose babies are they?" he screamed over and over like a mad man. Each time he asked the question, he stomped her in her back.

"Stop! Carlos, please stop!" she cried. "These are our babies. Please don't hurt our babies!"

Carlos snatched her up from the floor by her hair. He again slapped her into the door. Before she could move or even wrap her arms around her stomach, he kicked her hard in her abdomen. The pain that shot through her body was excruciating and moved the earth beneath her. An ear piercing scream came deep from within her throat. Jordyn felt as if she was bleeding inside. When she looked down her khaki pants were wet. A mixture of water and blood was running down her legs.

The monster just watched her. He finally realized what he had done. That's when all the lies of "I love you," "I'm sorry," and "it won't happen again," came. But this time, it was too late.

"Get me to the hospital!" Jordyn screamed. She was only six months pregnant but her water had broken.

Carlos carried her to the car. He turned on the flashers and drove at top speed to the hospital. Jordyn was in pain ,but she rubbed her belly and talked to her babies.

"It's going to be okay. I promise," she kept telling her girls. But everything wasn't okay.

Within the hour, her baby girls were born. She couldn't have been happier. But they were quickly rushed away. The doctor said that their lungs were not fully developed and they couldn't breathe on their own. They also had other complications, no doubt, as a result of the beating. He wasn't sure if there was anything they could do to save Jordyn's girls.

"I need a moment alone with Jordyn," Dr. Ford said to Carlos. Carlos simply nodded, offered Jordyn a smile, and left the room.

As soon as the door closed, Dr. Ford asked, "Who is responsible for your bruises?"

Jordyn didn't know what to say. The Carlos she loved was back. She didn't want him arrested.

"Jordyn, whoever beat you is responsible for you going into labor. Whoever did this to you is the reason your babies are fighting for their lives right now."

That person was Carlos, the father of her babies. She wanted to protect him but at what cost? He didn't mean more to her than her babies. Jordyn couldn't let him think that simply saying "I'm sorry" was going to make things okay. Her babies were forced to fight for every breath they took because of him.

She pointed towards the door. "It was my boyfriend. But, please, tell me my babies will make it. Do whatever you have to do!" she pleaded.

Dr. Ford took her hand in his. "We'll do our best but it's in God's hands." At the door he turned around and gave her a hopeful smile. "And I'll take care of the young man."

Jordyn's parents arrived shortly after. They were confused. They told her that Carlos had called them and when they got there the police were taking him away in handcuffs.

"What's going on, Princess?" her father asked.

She didn't want to but it was time for Jordyn to tell her parents about the silent hell she lived in for the past year. They couldn't believe their ears when she told them of all the pain Carlos had inflicted on her. David wanted to kill him. Lorraine held her daughter closely.

Moments later, Dr. Ford and a nurse returned with her babies. Both looked gloomy. Tears were in their eyes and tears sprang from Jordyn's eyes.

"We've tried but there's nothing we can do." Dr. Ford was almost in tears. "We want you to spend this time with them."

The nurse handed Jordyn both baby girls. The doctor and his nurse left the room.

Jordyn, David, and Lorraine watched the little girls as they struggled for every breath. As much as they were suffering, Jordyn could have sworn she saw smiles on their faces when it was over. They seemed to have slipped away at the exact same moment. With the end of their lives, a big part of Jordyn's life ended. And when the girls died, a part of Jordyn died.

She heard her parents praying silently but she didn't join them. She had prayed.

She prayed and asked God to perform a miracle. But there was no miracle. God didn't listen to her prayer. Instead, He took away her babies.

"No!" Jordyn screamed after kissing her girls good bye. "No!"

She didn't realize she was actually screaming in her sleep. Somehow she had dozed off and was dreaming about that day. Her parents ran in to check on her. She assured them that she was just having a bad dream.

"Want to talk about it?" Lorraine had offered, consoling her daughter as only a mother could.

Jordyn shook her head. She didn't want to talk about it. Jordyn just wanted her babies. Talking about it wasn't going to bring her babies back. God had taken them away from her.

In the weeks that followed the burial, Jordyn dreamed of her children. She smelled their sweet baby smell. She held the girls close to her heart. But with the dawn of a new day came the harsh reality of truth.

Morning after morning, Jordyn would awaken only to discover her beautiful babies were not in her arms. But she could still smell them so she would search for her babies only to find empty cribs. Realizing that they were not there, she still did not have the heart to take the cribs down. As far as Jordyn was concerned, those cribs were to never be taken down. It would finalize the reality that her twins would never come home.

Jordyn would go for days without eating. She simply didn't have an appetite. Then she would binge for twenty-four hours straight hoping to find comfort in the candy bars, chips, and ice cream she gorged. But not even the food could console her. Once a size sixteen Jordyn, put on at least fifty additional pounds. She could no longer fit into her clothing. She could barely wear her mother's size twenty clothing.

A grueling year of depression followed the burial of the twins, Brytnee Zakiya and Breeanna Zanaye. Jordyn found very little consolation in the fact that Carlos was only sentenced to one year in prison. Her heart was broken for eternity.

She wished she could go back and feel her girls being born again. Everyday she wished for them to have a second chance at life. She remembered the way they looked. When they were born they reminded Jordyn of little tan, furless kittens. They had beautiful silky, curly hair and the longest eyelashes Jordyn had ever seen. Jordyn longed for her precious babies so much. She felt them as she held herself. Jordyn imagined them still in her arms.

Pain
This pain rains on me everyday of my life.
Life as I once knew it no longer exists.
Pain is all I see and it is all that I know.
Pain is my only friend.
Pain has remained by my side throughout this entire ordeal.
Thank you Pain, thank you.

Two weeks after graduation, Jordyn began working at Dunkin Donuts. She made an effort to get along with everyone. She also put forth a lot of effort to communicate with others.

This once, over-opinionated sista, now had to learn to communicate all over again. It devastated her. But little did she know that life was about to change.

It was at her new job that she met Eric Carter and her life as she knew it changed. Jordyn began smiling often and not really knowing why. She stopped dressing in all black. She finally lost enough weight to fit into her own stylish wardrobe that consisted of vibrant colors. She started styling her hair differently daily, just like she had done before the loss of her twins. It was as if her soul opened up and let the sunshine back in. Jordyn had been reintroduced to life. She became reacquainted with joy. She could not have been happier.

"Hey Beautiful." Those were the first words that Eric spoke to Jordyn. Just his words along with his smile opened up a small window inside of her. Away went some of her pain.

"Hey," she responded. "Can I take your order?" she asked the stranger nervously.

"Well, what I would really like is to take you out." Unlike her he wasn't shy.

Jordyn had not been out on a date in a long time. The last steady boyfriend she had was her twin's father, the monster.

"I...I guess that would be nice," Jordyn answered. The two began dating a few

evenings later and soon became inseparable. Eric would even go to the cemetery with her and sit for hours while she visited her angels.

Eric Carter was twenty-five years old. He was a father to two very energetic and outgoing children. His son, Kelvin Terrell, was six years old. His daughter, Eriana Shanaye, was four and quickly became the apple of Jordyn's eye. Eriana reminded Jordyn of herself as a little girl. Eriana always made Jordyn laugh, even when she did not want to. Looking at Eriana, Jordyn began to remember her own girls with a smile instead of tears. The short memories that Jordyn had of her girls no longer made her cry. She began to remember her girls with joy and a smile.

Eric was so kind and compassionate. He may not have been the greatest intellectual, but so what? He was good to her and good for her. Because of him, she felt alive again. Even after losing the weight and fitting into her own clothes, Jordyn still was not happy with herself. Eric saw the beauty in her that she still could not see in herself. That was all that mattered to Jordyn. After a year of depression, she was finally able to live beyond the pain that had consumed her whole.

Eric proposed only six months after meeting Jordyn. "I know we haven't known each other long, but I love you." His words brought tears to her eyes. "Jordyn, will you marry me?"

She happily screamed her answer, "Yes!" With joy in her heart she wrote this poem for Eric Jamaal Carter, her husband to be.

Because Of You
Because of you,
my world is now whole.
Because of you,
love lives in my soul.
Because of you,
I have laughter in my eyes.
Because of you,
I am no longer afraid of good-byes.
You are my pillar,

my stone of strength.
With me through all seasons,
and great times of length.
My love for you is pure,
boundless through space and time,
it grows stronger everyday
with the knowledge that you will always be mine.
At the altar,
I will joyously say "I do,"
for I have it all now,
and its all because of you

Jordyn had the infamous Mischa, the local fashion designer, create her dream wedding gown. Jordyn designed it herself. It had a halter top with a beautiful, classy neckline. The beading was absolutely beautiful. There were ivory pearls and rhinestones that sparkled like diamonds. Jordyn even had Mischa design Eriana a matching flower girl gown. The bridal party would wear Jordyn's favorite color, pink.

Jordyn finally felt like the princess that her father, David, had always said she was. David had always tried his best to make her feel the way that she felt now. He was so happy to see his princess smiling. He did not even think twice about the cost of the wedding, which climbed steeper by the day.

As her special day came closer, she began to realize that she was no longer dreaming. This level of love and happiness was actually possible. Finally, a dream was coming true for Jordyn DeAsia Thomas. She was living life again. And as much as she missed her twin girls, she was happy to be back in the world of the living.

Eric and Jordyn's wedding was so touching and sweet. You could feel the love the minute you stepped into the church. She even wrote special vows just to recite to Eric and the children, Kelvin and Eriana.

She stared deeply into the eyes of the man who had breathed life back into her. She loved him so dearly and felt so indebted to him. She spoke softly for his ears only, carefully enunciating every word that traveled from her full lips to his awaiting ears.

I Promise
"I promise to love you Eric with all my soul.
Kelvin, I promise to always support you
at your little league games. Eriana I will always
Be around to listen to you sing and watch you dance.
Family I love you all with my very being.
I promise.

But life is not a fairy tale. It takes more than a man to uplift a woman. Man is imperfect and just as sure as Jordyn felt Eric took her pain away; it was he who brought even more pain into her life. A pain that overfilled her already bruised heart.

Despite the fact that the once charming Eric had become verbally abusive shortly after their vows, six months into their marriage, Jordyn was happily carrying his baby. She was only six weeks, but she was so very excited. She was already spending her days dreaming up baby names. Her favorite was, ZaNyiah

Lorrayna. The middle name was derived from her mother's first name, Lorraine.

Jordyn had gotten off from work at the library where she worked part time. She went to pick the kids up from the after school program at the Y.W. C. A. She took them to her maternal grandmothers for the evening. She then went to pick up dinner from Eric's favorite restaurant, Boston Market. She was so excited. She could not wait to go home and share her news with Eric.

When she arrived at home, there was a strange car parked in the driveway. She just assumed that the car belonged to one of Eric's buddies. No big deal. She was sure that as soon as she leaned over and kissed Eric's ear lobe seductively, the friend would be sent away. It was their evening. Hopefully, he would be as excited as she was and they would make love all night. Her body missed his touch.

She unlocked the door with a sultry grin on her face. Jordyn set their dinner on the kitchen table and proceeded into the living room. She heard an unfamiliar female voice. The woman's voice had a soft, but extremely country bumpkin drawl to it.

Jordyn entered the living room. At first they didn't even notice her. They were just sitting there laughing and having a good time watching Jordyn's favorite sitcom, "Good Times."

Jordyn cleared her throat and introduced herself to the woman. "I'm Jordyn Carter, Eric's wife. And you are?" she asked as she extended her hand to shake the other woman's. The older, unattractive, Caucasian woman barely spoke a word to Jordyn and did not return her smile. Her gut feeling told her that this woman was the source of the hang up that started two months into their marriage.

"Eric, aren't you going to introduce your *friend?*" Jordyn was surprised at the calmness in her own voice. She wanted to tear the woman apart. Only she knew better than to put the life of her unborn child at risk.

"Erma and I work together," Eric answered. His voice cracked and he refused to make eye contact with either woman. Jordyn suddenly felt sick to her stomach. He was lying to her.

"Excuse me!" the burly woman exclaimed angrily. She then said to Jordyn, "I'm not just his co-worker or friend. I'm his lover!" She was quite cocky.

Jordyn heard what the woman said and she knew in her gut that the words were true. But Jordyn turned to Eric. She had to hear what he had to say. "Is this true, Eric?"

Eric looked at Jordyn without compassion and replied, "I'm leaving you for Erma." Immediately, tears spilled out of Jordyn's eyes. "Leaving me?" Jordyn asked. "You

really think that I'm just gonna sit back and watch you walk out with this ugly Thing?" Jordyn balled up her fist and began swinging wildly at both Eric and his lover.

Eric was trying to grab her but she was a woman scorned. The more he tried to retain

her, the harder she fought. She heard his lover scream every time a punch landed.

"You can't just walk in here and take my husband!" Jordyn yelled.

Eric finally managed to wrap his arms around her, holding down her arms. Erma ran from the apartment crying and yelling. Jordyn yelled behind her, "This ain't over! Don't no woman come into my house and try to take what's mine!"

Eric didn't offer an explanation so Jordyn finally asked, "Why, Eric? What did I do wrong?" Jordyn was thinking over their short marriage. She took good care of the kids. She cooked every day. The apartment was always clean. Even though Eric barely touched her anymore, she was always ready and willing when he did want intimacy.

"I shouldn't have married you. You're just too young. We can't have a future together." *What does age matter now?* Jordyn wondered. They loved each other so much and she needed him. Their kids needed him. The life inside of her needed him.

"But Eric! I have some important news to share with you!" Jordyn cried as she felt him slipping away. He released her and headed for the door. He was going behind Erma. Jordyn

ran behind him, screaming, "Eric, no! Eric, you can't leave me. I've got some important news! Eric, please!"

He heard her screams. He even pushed her away every time she got close enough to grab hold of his arm. Eric climbed into the passenger seat of Erma's Chevy Lumina and locked the door as Jordyn approached him. She was out of breath and crying hysterically. "Eric!" she screamed his name over and over as she pounded on the window and door. But her cries fell on deaf ears. Eric and Erma sped away. Jordyn was left alone in the dark driveway.

The week that followed Eric's leaving was the most traumatic thing that Jordyn had experienced since the twins passed. The stress and pain of the only man she had ever really loved, other than her father, rejecting her for another woman, was too much. It was more than her heart and her baby could handle. At only seven and a half weeks into her pregnancy Jordyn had a severe miscarriage.

With the death of her unborn baby, along with the loss of her stepchildren, whom she loved as if they were her very own, Jordyn fell deeper into depression than she ever had before. She even contemplated suicide. Only one thing stopped her from committing suicide. The thought of her parents and just how truly hurt they would be to find her dead the next day. She could not bear the thought of causing them so much pain.

Jordyn suffered silently. Only she knew of her miscarriage. No one else knew that she had once again lost a part of her own being. There was no funeral this time. This time there was just a medical procedure that she endured on her own. After it was over and nothing of her pregnancy remained, other than her memories, Jordyn went home to an empty house that matched the empty life that had become hers once again. And this time she didn't even have a real job. She had no idea how she would pay her bills from month to month.

If things weren't bad enough, she was notified that they owed close to one thousand dollars in back rent. Eric told her that he had been paying the rent monthly. But as it turns out, Jordyn was facing eviction unless she could prove that the rent had been paid.

Jordyn searched Eric's empty drawers for receipts. Instead of finding a receipt, she found a small bag that contained a white, powdery substance. She shook her head in denial. It couldn't be what she thought it to be. Cocaine? How could she live with and love Eric all this time and not know that he was using drugs. That explained the rent not being paid. It also explained his severe and sudden mood swings. Jordyn felt so stupid as she flushed the narcotics down the toilet. If she could have, she would have flushed herself down the drain as well.

It took every dime of Jordyn's savings to pay the rent and secure the apartment for two more months. Then she had to do what she did not want to do. She had to go to her parents and ask them for money. That meant finally admitting that her marriage was over because her husband, the drug addict, had left her for another woman. It was so embarrassing to share that with her parents but they never judged her. They gave her what she needed and assured her that she could count on them for anything.

The months that followed the end of her marriage and her miscarriage were dark. Jordyn spent most of her days inside with the blinds drawn. She ignored the ringing phone. Most of the time it was Eric calling to ask her for either money or sex. She refused to give him either. It was hard to let him go but it was harder to try and restore the trust that he had snatched away. Because of him she had lost her third child.

Jordyn almost laughed at the irony. When she had first met Eric she was so grateful because she felt he had brought happiness back into her life. And now he was the reason that she was even more depressed than before. The man she had loved more than she loved even her own self had snatched the sunshine right out of the sky, leaving her world both cold and dark.

"Eric hurt you because you allowed him to."

Jordyn had no idea where the voice was coming from. She was all alone in her apartment. Not even the television was on. She looked around but no one was there.

"All you ever had to do was come to Me, Jordyn. I've always been here for you."

This time Jordyn knew exactly where the voice had come from. The voice had come from inside of her. God was speaking through her heart. She blamed only Eric for her pain but was she just as responsible?

Eric didn't take her out of the church or turn her against God. Jordyn could only blame herself for that. Her parents tried to encourage her to come back to church all the time. Jordyn declined. She wasn't sure why until that very moment. She had shut God out of her life when He took her twins away. And after just one year in prison, Carlos was free. Jordyn had stopped trusting in God. She had placed her trust in man. Jordyn's happiness had been in Eric's hands.

When she was depressed the first time, Jordyn didn't seek joy in the Lord. She thought that she had found it in Eric. He wasn't like Carlos. He didn't break her with his fists. No, he broke her with words that cut through her heart like a knife. She had entrusted her happiness to Eric alone. Jordyn had allowed her joy as she knew it to come through Eric.

Jordyn fell down on her knees and prayed to her Father. She was ready to feel the joy from within.

Father God

Father, I stretch my hands to thee.
Lord, I need you. Jesus I need to feel your
Spirit within my heart, within my soul.
Lord I need you to make me whole.
I want to be whole again, in your name
I need you. Oh Lord I need you. I need to feel you from
the top of my head to the soles of my feet.
I need you. God you blessed me with life. My own.
I am sorry that it took so very long for me to see,
For I refused to see what You see in me.
Lord, thank You for your love and your mercy and grace.
Lord, I just thank You just for who You are.
My God, You have been so very good to me.
Even when I wasn't good to myself.
You loved me before I even knew me.
And Lord, I just thank You.
Thank You for all that You are
And all that You do.
In Your son, Jesus Christ's name I pray,
Amen

Jordyn finally realized the greatest loves of her life. God the father, first and foremost, followed by herself, her parents, and her love of poetry. Jordyn realized she had a strong will to live and to succeed in life. Never again would she turn her back on her Father or put her happiness in someone else's hands. As her mother had said many times, "God makes no mistakes. Even when we hurt, He knows what's best. We just have to trust in Him and believe in his love for us."

God answered her prayer for renewal and granted her the ability to discover the joy within herself. Jordyn began to like how it felt to appreciate her inner beauty. She started to like herself. It felt almost as good as GOD is. She sat down to pen her appreciation to the man who really loved her. She called Him awesome, but many know Him as God.

Appreciation

I've had to learn to love me from every angle.
From the top of my head to the soles of my wide feet.
From the thickness of my belly, to the curious look in my eyes.

To the fullness of my face and the kiss of my smile.

I had to learn to love me the way God has always loved me.

Appreciatively.

Thank You God, for loving me!!!

A Mother, Her Son, and The Father
Fon James

"Ms. Alana, you have a call holding on line four," Misty's squeaky voice protruded out of the telephone.

"Okay, I'll pick it up in just a minute."

"Ms. Alana, it's Courtney calling and she sounds very upset. I think you may want to pick up right away."

Courtney Phillips was Alana's *pretend* daughter-in-law. Her son McCall had been seriously dating *his new love* Courtney for six months, but they had been friends for years. The two didn't waste anytime getting to know each other better. Actually, Courtney was McCall's pregnant girlfriend. She and Alana had developed a good relationship, as Alana did with all of her only son's love interests. She raised him to be a respectable young man, but without a father in his life, there was only so much a mother could teach him.

Alana scratched her head and looked at the clock. *What in the world could this girl be calling me about now*, she wondered. Courtney had a habit of calling Alana all throughout the day to talk about the baby kicking or any movement the baby was making. You would think this wouldn't be such a big deal since she already had two kids! But she was the love of McCall's life, so Alana obliged her call every time. But this calling every hour was beginning to get on her nerves. As the assistant operations manager and the only black woman in an executive leadership position for Houston company, Hathaway Oil, she needed to be on her P's and Q's at all times. The *light-skinned* people always seemed to be breathing down her neck and it took nothing short of a miracle and much prayer to make it through each day without having to explain every decision she made.

She decided to pick up the phone. "Alana Mitchell speaking," she answered in the most professional voice she could muster. She didn't want Courtney to think she had a lot of time to waste today.

"Mom, it's Courtney! I don't know where McCall is!"

Alana slowly reclined back in her black leather office chair and peered out the wall-length window at Buffalo Bayou below. *This little girl has got to be trippin' right? She is not calling me talking about she doesn't know where my son is*, she thought. In a relaxed voice, she responded to Courtney's antics very slowly.

"Courtney, sweetie, I am at work. Okay? I don't have time to keep up with my twenty-five-year-old-son and his whereabouts. I am sure he will call you soon if you haven't been able to reach him, okay sweetie?"

"Mom, no you don't understand." Courtney paused, "he, he, he went to meet with this guy about getting his money back for those rims he bought me for my car, but he hasn't come back yet. That was three hours ago and I haven't been able to reach him on his cell phone. That's not like McCall, Mom! He always answers when I call him. Mom, please, I don't know what to do or what to think." She pleaded.

"Okay, Courtney, please stop crying, girl. I am sure he is fine. Let me try to call him from my cell phone. Hold on, okay?" Alana pressed the mute button.

This boy and his women really do work my nerves. I know he will answer if he sees my number. He was probably fooling around with Melodie or something. Even though they were no longer a couple, for some reason he couldn't leave Melodie alone. It probably had to do with the fact that he was still in love with her. Alana really liked Melodie, but whomever her son wanted to date was his business.

The voicemail came on.

"Call, this is Momma, give me a shout when you get the message, honey. You got your crazy girlfriend crying over here wondering where you are and calling me at work. Give her a call or give me a call back. Love you honey. Bye."

Alana picked her office phone back up and pressed the mute button.

"Courtney, I didn't get any answer, but I am sure he is fine. Who did he go to meet again?"

"Some guy name Loco or Loca. Shoot, I don't remember. I can't believe I don't remember what his name is!" Courtney answered.

"Courtney would you please calm down and just give it a minute, I am sure he will call. You know how men are. They get to talking like us women and lose track of time. Speaking of losing track of time, I have a meeting in about 5 minutes that I need to go to. Call me back when you hear from him, okay?"

"But Mom, this isn't like him. He always, always answers my call no matter what he is doing."

Yeah right, unless he is doing somebody else. she thought, snickering aloud. She regained her composure so Courtney wouldn't hear her laughing. "Well look, baby, he's a grown man and he knows how to take care of himself. So you stop worrying your pretty little head before you have my grandbaby prematurely. I'll call you when I get out of my meeting if I haven't heard from you by then, which I know I will."

Alana grabbed her blackberry and sent her son a text message: HONEY, PLS CALL THAT PREGO GF OF YOURS. SHE IS WORRIED AND SO I AM FOR THAT MATTER. HEADED TO A MEETING. LOVE YOU, MOMMA.

❧ ❧ ❧ ❧ ❧

It was three in the afternoon before Alana got back to her desk from her meeting with the executive management team at Hathaway. While she loved her job and being a pioneer for African-American women, she really didn't like the culture of the company. Hathaway was an oil and gas company that had been around for many years. It was one of the first start-ups during the big oil boom in Houston, and it was now owned by big time oil tycoon, J.S. Calahan.

Alana was the first African American to be on the executive leadership team. While Hathaway liked to portray the image of diversity in their marketing materials and with the press, it was very evident from meetings like the one she just left, that all are not happy about her being there. Alana didn't care though. She was a force to be reckoned with and even though she didn't like playing their game, she liked winning at it. She was a forty-six year-old single mother who beat the odds. With so many hurdles women of color have to jump, Alana not only graduated from college, raised her only son, enrolled back in college after working for a while, she earned an MBA in less than two years. She was the first woman and the first Black woman to reach a prominent position in what some would call one of the oldest "good ole boy" networks in Houston. Even though she was a petite woman standing at a mere five-foot-four with her power heels and the leg lengthening signature pinstriped power suits she donned everyday, she could definitely hold her own.

Her message light was red, so she pressed the AUDIX button to retrieve her messages. The robotic sounding computer woman announced: "You have 9 messages."

"Oh my goodness! Why do I have all these messages on my phone?" She then remembered that her secretary Misty left early today for a dentist appointment.

She took out her pen and notepad to write each one down. Without Misty screening her calls, she would have to do it herself today. She pressed the speakerphone button and turned up the volume.

Message One at 1:02 p.m. "Mom, it's Courtney, I still have not heard from McCall. Please call me back."

Message Two at 1:08 p.m. "Mom, It's Court, still nothing. I don't know what to do. I am going crazy over here. Call me back please."

Message Three at 1:29 p.m. "Okay Mom, you know this ain't like him not to call us back. Please can you call me or something. Guess you **are** probably in a meeting. I'll call you back later."

Message Four at 1:35 p.m. "Oh yeah, Mom, the baby is kicking **big time**. You think that's a sign or something? Call me back."

By now Alana had had enough of this. If all nine calls were from Courtney, she was going to kill that girl the next time she saw her.

Message Five at 1:55 p.m. "Mom, it's McCall. I—"

Alana replayed the message. *What was all that noise in the background?* she wondered? It sounded like a lot of wind, but it was so quick, she really couldn't decipher what it was. She concluded that his call must have dropped. She knew that his janky cell phone was always dropping calls. She proceeded to listen to the next message, figuring it would be McCall calling right back.

Message Six at 2:02 p.m. "Alana, this is Bill. Give me a call would you. I want to go over those numbers you presented in the meeting again. Something just didn't quite jive well with me and I wanted to make sure you calculated everything correctly. Thanks, Alana."

Alana rolled her eyes. "Didn't quite jive well with me," she mocked. "Humph, he has big nerves and he's not even in operations. He's in another department. This isn't even his area of expertise. It's mine!" Alana felt herself getting perturbed. It was time for her daily talk.

"Lord, it's Alana again. Please help me not to lose it up in here. I know we have this conversation everyday, sometimes four and five times a day, but I need you to help strengthen me to deal with these people here. It's hard sometimes, Father, it really is."

God spoke to Alana's spirit. *"My sweet Alana. I know it's hard, but I put you there because I know you can handle it. You are making a difference in this place and I have to keep you here for my will to be done. You can make it my child. You can make it. Just remember who you really work for."*

Alana wasn't just saved, she knew the Lord intimately. She had a relationship with Him, and throughout all of the adversities she had faced in her life being a single mom with a young son, and often times struggling her way to the top in a corporate world that didn't really invite her in, she knew that her relationship with God was the only thing throughout the years that helped her continue to reach higher ground. While her son wasn't always doing the right thing, she knew that he knew Jesus Christ as his Savior. He was young and she always prayed to God that he would straighten up his life when it came to women. He was fine in other areas of his life and often attended church with her, but women were his downfall. Alana thought when he met Melodie, he would settle down and everything would be better, but he has continued to go back and forth between his love for God and his love for another kind of intimacy; sex.

She refocused and started listening to her messages again.

Message Seven at 2:17 p.m. "Okay, Mom, please call me." Courtney cried heavily on the phone. "Mom, I called that guy that, that, that Mc, McCall was going to meet and he said, he, he said, he, he said he hasn't seen him," she panted. "He's lying Mom, I just know he is. Why would he lie like that? Please call me back!" Courtney crjed and stuttered.

Message Eight at 2:35 p.m. "Ms. Alana Mitchell, this is Mr. Allen with the *Chronicle*. I wanted to discuss your role in Hathaway Oil and where you see yourself in the next few years as the lone black woman in a corporate world plentiful of white men." Laughter erupted through the phone. "Hey Lani, it's just Sterling. I hope you haven't forgotten about our dinner date tonight. Call me baby when you get a minute. Wanted to make our dinner reservations and I wasn't sure what kind of dining you wanted to partake of tonight. Did you like my little joke, hun? Call me and let me know."

Alana laughed. *He is so silly*. She was so happy to have Sterling. God had sent her a good saved man in Sterling Allen. They were introduced by mutual friends and had been hanging tightly together ever since. Her son even liked him and that was different because McCall never liked anyone that she dated. But for some reason, Sterling had won him over. Sterling had even changed church memberships and was now a part of the servant team at Alana's church, New Faith Horizon. He was a fine specimen of a man and God knew exactly who she needed.

He encouraged her, they worked out together, and just enjoyed being with each other. Most of their friends always joked with them about when they would exchange nuptials, but Alana knew that in due time, God would work that out too.

Message Nine at 2:55 p.m. "Mom, where are you? Please call me. Something had to have happened to McCall. He's nowhere to be found. None of his friends have heard from him. I love him, Momma, I love him so much. He's McNab's father." Courtney sniffed before the phone call ended.

"Lord, have mercy! What in the world is going on today?" Alana was about to dial McCall's phone when her office phone rang.

"Hey there sweetie. You get my message?"

"Hey handsome. Yes I got your message, but if you don't mind I need to call you back. Courtney has been blowing up my phone because she can't find McCall. I got a semi-message from him myself, but he hasn't returned any of my calls either."

"Okay, baby. That doesn't sound like McCall. What did he say?"

"It just basically said, 'Mom, it's McCall. I—,' then the phone hung up. There was a lot of noise in the background, but it was so quick. I really couldn't pick up on what it was. I am really starting to get worried now. He was supposed to be meeting with some guy about rims, but Courtney left me a message saying the guy says he never saw him. I hope nothing bad has happened to my baby."

"Don't even think that sweetie. I am sure McCall is okay. He probably lost his phone or laid it down somewhere. Who knows, the battery just may be dead. That would explain why the call cut off and he hasn't called anyone back yet."

"Yeah, you're right, honey. He's fine. He's a big boy," she laughed. "I'm just hoping he's not over there with Melodie because I am not covering for his butt if Courtney finds out. She'll be kicking him all up and down the streets while pregnant!"

They both laughed at the thought of Courtney whipping up on McCall.

"Well, how about dinner tonight. What do you have a taste for?"

"Hmm, let me see. Oh, I know. Why don't we try that new Thai food place over in River Oaks? I hear it's really good."

"Thai food? Okay, okay, it's your choice. Not sure I would have chosen it, but like I said, whatever my baby wants, that's what she gets."

"Okay, Sterling, I'll see you at seven tonight." "Wear that black dress I bought for you last week while we were shopping at the Galleria. And the shoes I got you too. Aw shucks, just wear the whole outfit woman."

"Yes, dear. I had already planned to wear it anyway. See you tonight," she gushed.

Alana hung up the phone and dialed McCall's phone. It went straight to voicemail. "Sterling's probably right. His battery has gone down or something. Let me call Courtney and see if she is okay. Her and little McNab."

Alana really didn't like the name McNab, but it had grown on her. McCall insisted that his son's name be similar to his, and since he loved Donovan McNabb, the black quarterback for the Philadelphia Eagles, McNab became her future grandson's name.

Alana dialed Courtney's cell phone and she picked up on the first ring.

"Hello, Mom, have you heard from Call? Please tell me you have heard from him."

"I'm sorry sweetie, I haven't. He did leave me a short message that sounded like his phone may have cut off or something due to a bad signal. Maybe his battery is dead."

Courtney wanted to believe Alana, but she just couldn't shake this feeling that something bad had happened to him.

"Courtney, tell me again. Who did he go to meet with and where? I'll call around to see if anybody has seen him."

"I tried calling everybody we know, Mom, but nobody has seen him. His boys Jamal and Melvin are out looking for him now. Mom, if he doesn't call in the next few minutes, I am going to call the police. I am serious. Something ain't right about all this."

"Gurrrrl, please! McCall is alright. Don't even think the worse like that. My baby is fine and he knows how to take care of himself. Let's just pray and hope that he calls one of us soon or that Jamal or Melvin calls back with the good news that he's okay."

ۍ ۍ ۍ ۍ ۍ

"Dinner was great baby. This Thai stuff isn't bad at all," Sterling said, rubbing his stomach. "I am pretty full too, and I just knew for sure I would still be hungry. I can't wait for dessert. What kind of dessert do they serve in a place like this anyway," he chuckled.

"Yeah it was very good," Alana muttered dryly.

She still had not heard from McCall and this definitely wasn't like him. She tried pushing any bad thoughts out of her head. She prayed about it and relied on her faith. She knew McCall was in God's hands. She turned the ringer off on her cell phone for dinner with Sterling. She wanted to focus on having a good time with him. Work had been very crazy with Bill accessing every line item in her presentation. And to add insult to injury, her vice president Bob didn't even refute Bill's request when she mentioned it to him. "Just provide him with what he needs," he replied. She really hated the way they always undermined her work and her authority. It was a constant struggle on that job, but she always persevered. God never let her down. He was the reason she was still there and doing well, in spite of the obvious persistent backlash she faced daily.

"You okay sweetheart? Your mind seems preoccupied with something. Are you thinking about McCall? Why don't you just go ahead and call Courtney back? She's already called you a thousand times by now, I'm sure."

"I have to let McCall live his life. I can't go running around looking for him. Maybe he needed some time away or something. He's a grown man and he doesn't have to report to me or Courtney. I can't worry about him. I have to cut the apron strings. That's what you always tell me, 'Leave the boy alone Lani, let him be a man.' Remember that Sterling?" Alana mimicked his voice.

Alana peered at the phone in her purse. The light was blinking red signaling she had a message. "Sterling, I am going to go ahead and check my voicemail if you don't mind. Excuse me for a minute please."

Alana picked up her purse and headed toward the back of the restaurant toward the restroom. She figured she could kill two birds with one stone if she went ahead and used the restroom while she was back there. Her Thai iced tea had finally started to take its toll.

She finished up in the restroom and headed toward the door. She pressed her voicemail button as she was exiting the restroom. "You have one message. Press one to play the message." Alana pressed one. At first all she heard was crying and sniffling. Then she heard Courtney's voice, but it sounded very weak.

"Mom, it's Courtney. Please call me as soon as you get this message. Please Mom. I have to talk to you right now."

Alana immediately dialed Courtney's number. When Courtney spoke, Alana dropped the phone and fainted in the restroom.

෴ ෴ ෴ ෴ ෴

"Baby, are you okay? Baby, can you hear me? Lani, please honey, can you hear me?"

Alana could barely hear Sterling's voice, but she knew he was near. What was going on, she thought. Why couldn't she see clearly? Her vision was blurred and she could hardly hear. She knew Sterling was near because she could smell his signature *Aqua Di Gio* cologne. Everybody was talking around her. She heard someone say, "Bring the gurney over here. This is the lady that fainted."

Alana closed her eyes again. When she reopened them she was in a hospital bed. She looked around her. Her vision was still blurred. She saw Sterling's six feet tall, dark and muscular frame standing near the window talking to what looked liked the doctor. On her other side stood Courtney. *Where was McCall?*

She cleared her dry throat tried to sit up. Sterling and the doctor immediately turned their attention to her and they all rushed to her side.

"Where's McCall? Where is my son?" She didn't like the look that everyone was displaying. Grief-stricken faces greeted her. She turned to Courtney who was already started crying. Alana instantly sat up. "What is it? Where is he? Would somebody answer me?" Alana shouted. Her doctor asked her to calm down.

"Calm down, where's my son? Where's my McCall?" Alana began to cry. Why was she crying? She didn't really know, but her mother's intuition told her that something wasn't right. And why was she in the hospital if something was wrong with McCall. Was he in another room or something? She had to find out.

She tried to get out of the bed, but Sterling and the doctor held her down. She tossed and turned trying to get away, but to no avail.

"Honey, we have to tell you something, but we don't want to upset you because your blood pressure is very high right now and you are bordering dangerous levels."

"Sterling, please tell me what's going on!"

"Lani, I'm sorry to tell you this, but McCall is missing. When Courtney told you what happened, you fainted. The police are aware and they are looking for him now."

"What do you mean he's missing?" she queried.

"We can't find him, Lani. Nobody has heard from him since he went to meet with that guy about the rims. The police are looking for that guy right now to question him. I had my friends at the station push his missing case file to the top. I help them out a lot during my investigative reports for the paper, so they owed me a favor. Courtney provided a recent picture of him to the police for flyers. His friends are canvassing the area too."

Alana couldn't do anything. She just sat there and listened as Sterling filled her in. Tears were streaming down her face. She couldn't even fathom losing McCall. He was her only child. She was his mother. He was her son. She closed her eyes. She needed to connect with her heavenly Father.

"Lord, it's Alana again. I am not ready to lose my son. I know that you loaned him to me, but I can't lose him right now, please Lord, he is all I have. I know you have so much in store for him still, Lord. Please, wherever he is, let him be okay. Lord, please don't let him be in any pain. Father God, I need you right now more than I have ever needed you before. Please let them find him right now, Lord, in the name of Jesus. I love you, Lord. and you said you wouldn't put more on me that I could bare. Lord, I know that I can't bare life without McCall. Please Lord, please not this time Father."

All of a sudden, Courtney screamed and her water broke. Everybody looked in her direction..

"Oh my goodness, Courtney! You are not due for another two weeks!" Alana yelled. She tried getting out of bed, but the cords hooked up in her arm prevented her.

The doctor immediately called for a nurse. Sterling helped him place Courtney on the small gray guest sofa in the room. The nurse came in immediately with a wheelchair and Courtney was whisked off down the hall.

"Sterling, I have to go with her. That's my grandson. Oh my God, Sterling! Why is all this happening?" Alana cried.

"Baby, you can't go. I'll go and check on her. You need to stay calm and stay here. I'll have the nurse give you something to ease your anxiety."

"I don't need anything to ease my anxiety, Sterling! I need to make sure that Courtney and my grandson are okay."

Another nurse came in to calm Alana down. She inserted a drug into Alana's IV. Before she could remember what she was going to do next, Alana was out.

ॐ ॐ ॐ ॐ ॐ

"Ashes to ashes, dust to dust. We recommit his body back to the Lord," the minister spoke as rain pelted the tent. Everyone filed away from the baby blue casket.

The matching blue program had been filled with pictures recalling his extraordinary life. His picture was flanked by the words McCall Alan Mitchell. A loving son. A committed father. A loving friend. We will miss you Call.

"Don't cry McNab, it is okay baby. Your Daddy loves you so much." Alana said, holding McNab in her arms as she stood alone at her son's casket. "McCall, I know you were so excited about your son's arrival and I know you are looking down on us right now from heaven. I know you didn't want to leave us, but The Father commanded that you come home. We love you, son, and I know you are up there with God, making him laugh like you always made us laugh. I know that God took care of you when that man robbed you and took your life. I am so glad Call, that you knew God for yourself. I am at peace baby, because you were just on loan to me. I am so thrilled that God let me have you for twenty-five great years. I am happy that He allowed you to bless me with a beautiful grandson who already looks exactly like you. I love you son."

Alana kissed the casket and began to walk away from under the green tent. As she stepped out of the tent and headed toward the black limo, the sun began shining brightly and a rainbow appeared. During the ride over from the funeral, Alana had prayed and asked God to give her a sign that her beloved son was with Him. She had prayed, "Lord, thank you for my son and thank you for your son, Jesus. Father God, please show me *your* sun to let me know *my* son is now with *your son.*

Alana looked directly at the sun and then she kissed McNab. He smiled back at her. She knew that everything would be okay. God had never failed her and even though her son was no longer presently with her, he would always be with her in spirit. God had given her a great gift with her grandson and she was blessed that God thought enough of her to help her bare this loss with a beautiful gain.

When Alana got home, she realized that the messages from her home phone had not been checked in while. She clicked the play button.

"Mom, it's McCall. I got your message yesterday about Courtney getting on all your nerves calling you about McNab kicking and stuff," McCall laughed. "You are so silly. You know you love to hear every detail about your grandson. I love your crazy self, Momma, soon to be grandmomma. See ya later, okay?"

Alana smiled and thanked God for her last message from her son. She pressed the button and the voicemail said the word saved. She laughed and peered toward the ceiling. She knew that because she was saved and because McCall was saved, she would definitely see him later.

In Loving Memory of Rashad A. Smith.

DEATH AT A CHURCH
Jacqueline Moore

April could see the church on the horizon. She often passed by it at night when she was working. It always seemed so warm and inviting. She would listen to the soothing sounds of the choir practicing, late into the evening, as she strolled the block. Every now and then, one of the songs would stir something deep down within her soul; creating the need to fill a void that existed deep within her spirit, for as long as she could remember.

She didn't quite understand why hearing those songs saddened her. They were often happy and full of hope. Why did they bring tears to her eyes? April often wished she knew the answers to something she didn't even identify with. She didn't understand her feelings enough to try to explain them to her friends. They would just laugh at her and tell her how stupid she was. Yeah, her friends were good for that. Always reminding her of how dumb she felt when she tried to find the answers to questions everyone else seemed to know.

There was so much that she didn't know. However, rather than admit it, she hid it under a mask of defiance and bravado.

She was tired of her friends making her feel stupid all the time. She was forever on the outside looking in.

Although April referred to the women and men that she worked with as friends, she really didn't have any friends to speak of. She wasn't even sure what a friend was. There was no one she could depend on or share good times. Yes, they taught her things to help her survive when she walked these cold means streets by herself at night. However, April longed for a girlfriend whom she could just laugh and joke with. Someone she could ask real questions. Someone who could hold her hands when she felt scared, like she did right now. A true friend with whom she could share her innermost thoughts, hopes and dreams.

Well, this was it, April thought. She finally built up enough nerve to walk through the beautiful oak doors. Oh, how she admired those doors. Whoever created them obviously done so with great love and care. There was only one thing that she admired more: the endless stream of elegantly dressed and sophisticated women that always seemed to be going in and out of those very same doors.

April often wondered if she walked through those doors, would she come out the same way. Stunning and elegant, just like the women that she admired. She knew that it was only a dream. But a girl could dream, couldn't she? Still, she wondered what secrets lay behind those big beautiful doors and could she dare have the courage to go through with what she often dreamed about.

She had been on her own, living on the streets since the age of twelve. She remembered the day she finally decided to leave home. She was tired of being passed around like some piece of meat by her stepfather Kevin's friends. Her mother died of a drug overdose when she was seven years old, leaving her alone with her drug addicted husband. Since her mother was no longer around to service the men that would buy Kevin drugs, he started prostituting her instead. No matter how hard she tried, she would never forget the first time. Her mother wasn't even been buried yet when Kevin came up with his plan.

The man was old and smelly. His breath reeked of stale cigarettes and alcohol. He kept kissing her in her mouth as he held her down with thick greasy hands. He was too big for her to fight off. Besides, Kevin told her that if she didn't do what he said, he would leave her in the alley for the rats to feast on.

The room she stayed in was smelly, too. There was an old mattress that Kevin found in the alley that he dragged in and she used for her bed. She didn't have many clothes and always slept in what she had on. The stinky old man ripped the few buttons off the only blouse she had in his haste to undress her. The rest of her clothes were left bloody after the assault.

She was too scared to tell anyone. Besides, who would believe her? She was just a raggedy little girl with no mama and nobody to love her. She didn't even know who she could tell. Kevin's dope fiend friends? Not likely. They were as bad as him. When they weren't smoking crack, they used her for sex too.

April hadn't attended school since kindergarten. Even then, she only went for about a month. She and her mama never stayed in any one place long enough for her to go. Besides, she never saw any reason for her to learn to read and write anyhow.

Everyone was always telling her how stupid she was. It didn't make any sense for her to try to learn now.

Well, the time had finally come for her to try to learn a little something. She was tired of being alone and tired of men using her. She just wanted to find someone or something that would help her not to feel so sad and alone all the time. April just knew from all that she had seen and heard that maybe what she had been looking for lay just beyond the doors that stood in her way.

Slowly, she made her way up the stairs. She made sure that everyone had gone inside before she made her entrance. April had put on her best outfit, the one that everyone told her she looked good in. It was bright red and accentuated her best features, both in the front and in the back.

The choir was singing one of the soul stirring songs again. She stood just outside of the final door that would lead her to her destiny. Her heart pounded in her chest. Little by little, she pushed the door open. As she peered in, she could see that just inside the door where stood one of the ushers.

April was captivated by the melodic song that came from the front of the church. The beautiful harmony stirred up something deep within her heart as the song talked about sin and the precious lamb of God. Although April didn't know what inspiration was, she felt inspired by the words.

The usher's smile quickly faded as she slowly watched April enter. April had seen that look before. It was one of disdain. Women and even some men looked at her that way when she worked the corners late into the night. April hadn't expected to see that look in here.

Walking with her head down, April headed for the nearest seat at the back of the sanctuary. She was taken with the beauty of this place. There were awe inspiring paintings of places she had never seen before. At the front of the room, high above where everyone below was seated was a cross. There was a man on the cross with the saddest, yet most beautiful eyes that she had ever seen.

On his head sat some type of band that appeared to be covered with thorns. Blood trickled down his face, mixed with a look of sadness. The look reminded her of how she felt most of the time. April was mesmerized.

She was so caught up watching what was going up in front that she didn't noticed the ushers gathering together at the back of the church whispering to one another and pointing at her. April was entranced listening to the preacher that she didn't see that the couple who had been sitting right next to her slowly inched their way all the way to the opposite end of the pew.

The tears flowed from her eyes as she listened to the preacher talking about some man named Jesus, who was willing to forgive her if she would just ask Him to. April longed to meet such a man. She had never dared to dream of such a thing. She really didn't understand the meaning of the word forgiveness, but she knew it was something that she desperately wanted and desired.

At that moment, April wished she knew how to read. The man that was standing at the front of the church was talking about a woman who sold herself to men just like she did. The woman's name was Gomer, a prostitute who was redeemed by Hosea at the request of God. April longed to meet this man named God. She wanted to learn more about this woman and man.

April was so caught up in the sermon that when it was finally over, she didn't know what to do. However, what she did know was that she wanted to come back and learn more. She hadn't been this excited or happy for a very long time. Not since long before her mama had gotten hooked on drugs and died. There was also a new feeling that she had never experienced before: hope.

As she thought about all that she heard from the preacher, she felt that maybe her life really could be better. Maybe she could meet this Jesus who loved her in spite of every bad thing she had done.

The choir started singing again. There it was again, hope in the words of the song. Then she heard the preacher's words that spoke to her soul, "Come, if you want to know him. The doors of the church are open. I know there is someone here today who doesn't know him but wants to get to know him. Come forward."

As she slowly made her way to the front of the church, she felt everyone's eyes on her. Nervously looking around the pews, people were whispering about her. She paused for a moment and realized that the same beautiful women that she had admired from afar, look at her with contempt in their eyes. Their eyes were burning holes in her back. They made her feel dirty and unwanted.

She was about to turn around and run out of the church,when she felt someone's comforting and assuring arms grab her.

When the woman released her and looked into her eyes, April recognized it was a woman she saw on several occasions leaving the church after choir practice. The woman appeared about seventy years old, but you would never know it in the way she carried herself. April imagined that if she had a grandmother, she would want the woman to be her. With a welcoming and reassuring demeanor, the woman placed her arm around April's shoulder and led the rest of the way up the aisle.

"Now Sugar, don't let them devils keep you from meeting my God. Mama Nay's gotcha, honey. I ain't gonna let nobody mess witcha, child. Come on now, you can do this."

Mama Nay's voice was so soothing, it made April forget about the dirty looks that the other women sent her way. Slowly, she felt her courage returning. Yes, indeed, she wanted to meet Mama Nay's God.

What happened next was just a blur to April. All she knew was that she was finally going to meet him. The man she had heard so much about. Jesus. She knew that he would be able to help her. As they walked towards the back of the church, April could still feel the others staring at her. She was glad that Mama Nay was holding her hand. The excitement of it all was almost too much for her to handle.

They led the small group to a room just left of the sanctuary, where they had been sitting. April saw that she wasn't the only person who was interested in meeting this man called Jesus. There were two other women besides her. She wondered if they felt as uncomfortable as she did right now. One of the women couldn't have been much older than her and she could tell she didn't have to walk the streets for a living. April imagined the woman worked in a bank with her nice blue suit she wore to church. The older of the two had been crying. Her black mascara was streaked and her eyes looked like the eyes of a raccoon. April dared not laugh, but she wanted to.

The room they now found themselves in wasn't as beautiful as the sanctuary. It was a small room filled with a huge table and chairs and nothing else. They all sat down at a table. One of the ushers who had led them back there started passing around some papers for them to read and sign. April felt her heart drop. She didn't know she would have to sign something before she met Jesus. She hung her head in shame. It was the same old story. Everyone there would soon find out that she couldn't read or write.

She was about to get up and leave, she felt Mama Nay's reassuring hand on her shoulder once again. "What's the matter, Suga? Do you need some help?" April wanted to tell her what the problem was, but she couldn't open her mouth. She was too ashamed to tell this nice lady that she wouldn't be able to meet Jesus because she couldn't read the papers. Sensing what the problem was, Mama Nay took the papers off the table and started asking April questions so she could fill them out for her. April exhaled in relief. She was glad that the elderly and friendly woman had stayed by her side. Mama Nay provided something to April that she had never felt before in her life: comfort.

While answering the questions, April took the time to study the kindly woman who was so graciously helping her. Mama Nay was the kind of woman every child hoped her grandmother to be. She was the kind of woman April would dream of when she slept and silently prayed for brighter days. She had big strong arms to grasp you in a bear hug and a warm and inviting bosom that invited you to lay your head upon. Even her hands were made to hold and soothe a child who was hurt. She could pick you up, wipe away your tears, and comfort you in the same breath. Yes, April wished for a grandmother just like her.

The preacher entered the room as they were finishing the questions. He no longer wore his beautiful purple robe. He was simply dressed in a black suit with a white shirt and introduced himself as Pastor Jordan. April recognized his face as one she had seen on several occasions as she worked the streets at night. She tried on several occasions to convince him to spend a few dollars on her, but he always declined.

As Pastor Jordan stood in front of her to shake her hand, she saw the small trace of a smile on his lips. April wasn't really sure what the smile meant, but it did make her a little uncomfortable. As a matter of fact, men smiling at her always made her uncomfortable. April always saw the smile as a prelude to sex. She never spoken with a man who didn't want something from her.

She wondered if Jesus would want something from her too. The thought was fleeting as she realized it didn't matter. She was willing to do what ever was necessary to be forgiven. She wasn't quite sure what that meant, but she thought back to the story of Gomer. April could relate to her. Gomer wasn't like the other pretty women that were coming in and out of the church. April was sure they hadn't done anything like prostitute themselves to survive. The women who came to the church led nice quiet lives and didn't do anything wrong. She was sure of that. None of them had let men use their bodies the way she had. They didn't know what it was like to always feel stupid and alone. They couldn't know what it must be like to long for someone to just hold them and wipe away their tears when someone hurt them. No, these women didn't know how hard life could be. She was sure of that.

April started to believe that maybe she had made a mistake. The women in this place would never accept her once they realized what she had done. Suddenly, she got up out of her seat and started heading for the door.

Frantically, she paced, moving fast beyond each pew.

April was outside of the door, standing in the warm summer's sun, when Mama Nay finally caught up to her. "Chile, where ya going? I thought you wanted to meet Jesus." Mama Nay was out of breath as she spoke. April was ready to bolt down the street until she saw the sadness reflected in her new friend's eyes.

"Mama Nay, I can't go back in there. The women here won't ever accept me and I know that many of the men will hate me because I know their secrets. I don't belong here. This place is too nice for me. It wasn't meant for people like me." As she turned to walk away, April felt the strong grip of Mama Nay holding on for dear life.

"Daughter, this place was made for people just like you and me. Whatcha think? Everybody here all good ain't got no secrets? We all got secrets. Things we ashamed of. But we don't let that stop us from seeking God. Him da one who make it better. Him da one, who can make us better. Him da one who will forgive us and make us whole. Not the people you see inside."

As she finished speaking, April noticed that her new friend was crying too.

"Chile, when people look at you dey scared. Dey scared cause dey was either just like you, on da way to being you, or running away cause they afraid they knew someone just like you. We all gots things in our past we done want nobody to know about. We want errbody to think we always good and done right by God. Truth be told, ain't none of us ever done all good. Dere is bad in us all. Now listen when Mama talk, cause she know where she talk from."

April found herself sitting on the steps of the church, just the two of them, totally enthralled with every word coming out of the old woman's mouth. She listened as her new friend told her of her youth. She too had found herself left all alone, after her parents had died soon after coming to America from the Islands.

Mama Nay told her how she didn't know anyone and how people laughed at her when she went looking for a job. They laughed at how she looked and how she sounded when she spoke. Mama Nay told her about her life on the streets and how she had to sell her body just to eat. April was dumbfounded and couldn't believe what she was hearing. This sweet old lady had been where she was now.

Mama Nay told her about her own inability to read and write. How dirty and useless she felt. She knew all the pain April was experiencing. But most of all, she knew how to help April, the same way someone helped her all those years ago. She could help April by helping her find Jesus, if she would let her.

April knew at that moment, she was dead to her old life and looking forward to being born again. She knew that God had been calling to her and that He had placed her very own angel in her life to help her through. The April of old had died at the church that day and the new April was born, with a little help from a friendly old woman named Mama Nay.

HE LOVES US, ALWAYS
Linda Wattley

This morning, I had the strangest feeling my life would never be the same. Feelings we have deep down, where we know the inevitable is upon us. That's what came over me; mind, body and soul.

"Hey you! Keep the car today, honey, I'm riding with Lionel," Bob said as he put on his jacket, which covered his beautifully formed and muscular body and walked quickly down the stairs. People were in awe from such a wonderful physic. He was indeed the typical Bob, a person everybody loved to have around. His humor lingered when he would leave any setting. He had staying power.

"Okay, I will pick you up from work then," I said as I sat up in bed and wiped the sleep from my eyes. By that time, Robert and Marcus had climbed in bed with me.

The September autumn breeze embraced us as we got in the car. Our first mission was to pick up my grades from my final exams from Medical Assistant School. I had to see if I made the Honor Roll. I did! I could not wait to share the news with Bob. He was always so supportive of me and my career goals. We got in the car and continued our errands. We had two hours before we would pick up Bob, so I stopped by my Mom's house to share the good news. As we pulled up in her driveway, we heard the telephone ring.

"Lyn, it's for you. It's Bob," my Mom said as she handed me the phone. Still a beautiful woman, even at fifty, and not one spot of gray in her hair. She was barely five feet tall, and had become pleasingly plump in her older years.

"Hi Bob, we just got here. How did you know we were here?"

"I felt you were there. How are you and my boys?

"We're good. I finally made the Honor Roll," I said with excitement in my voice.

"Good for you! I've always been proud of you baby, and the mother you are to our kids."

"Thanks, Bob," I said as I began to feel he was so far away.

"Don't pick me up. Meet me at the house and we'll take the boys to get some ice cream."

"We were looking forward to coming to get you," I said, disappointed in the change of plans.

"I have something to do first. I'm going to get me some money then I am going to get you some money."

"What do you mean by that?" I asked with concern.

"Don't worry. I just called to say I love you and will see you soon."

The phone went dead after that. I turned and looked at my Mom with a perplexed look on my face. I grabbed my purse and told the boys, "We'll meet Daddy there."

"What's wrong, Lyn?" My Mom questioned.

"Oh, nothing I hope. I am just a little worried about Bob," I responded with a knot in the pit of my stomach.

The sun was beginning to go down, creating a beautiful scene in the sky as the sun prepared the sky for the moon. Robert, Marcus and I got home. They went up to their rooms to play while we waited for Bob. Suddenly, the stillness in the house was interrupted with a stern knock on our front door.

"Mrs. Jackson?"

"Yes, I am Mrs. Jackson."

"Ma'am, we just left the scene of a vehicular accident involving your husband," The officer said, finding it hard to look me in the eyes.

"Where is he?" I panicked.

"We had him sent to Akron City Hospital. You have to get there right away."

"Thank you," I said as my heart started pounding with an agony I've never known. Looking up towards the stairs, I became concerned about my sons having to share the next phase of this reality unfolding in our lives. I stood there, not wanting to move anywhere in time. I just wanted to freeze this moment in time and let life pass me by. Life as I knew it, was going to change forever, was the feeling I had in my gut, and I thought it was the reason for my drop in my spirit this morning. I violently shook my head, "No!" as I screamed aloud.

Robert was my four year old, who shared the same birthday as my husband; September 25th. This can not be happening. Marcus was two years old. Our lives were finally coming into harmony. Bob and I were growing up, and we were about to celebrate our sixth year of marriage the following month. This could not be happening. I needed more time to show Bob how much I loved him. He deserved to know that I finally got it. I finally understood love. You see, he always loved me for who I was. His face always lit up when he saw me. At first, I did not understand because I did not understand love. He taught me what love was all about. I was ready to be the wife he deserved to have.

"Not now, Lord!" I cried. I was finally freed from the demons of my past. My molested experiences of the past were finally being dissolved. He saw me through it. His love healed me. He is the only man that deserved the woman I had become. He can't leave me now. Oh God, no! Please do not take this man away from me. I beg you.

I had to have hope. I got my neighbor to take me to the hospital. My friend a couple of houses down, kept the boys while I went to check on their father.

I was dropped off in front of the Emergency entrance. Looking up to the sky, I prayed to God to not take my husband. With no hesitation, God told me to pray for something else, he is already gone. God's response shocked me. God never lied to me before, so by the time I reached the front desk, I was falling apart inside. Tears flooded my eyes, making my vision blurry, just as blurry as my judgment as anger immediately filled my being as I prepared to see my husband.

"My husband was just brought here. Robert Jackson, Jr.," I said frantically.

"Mrs. Jackson, the doctor will be out to see you. Do you have anyone with you?"

"No," I yelled quietly, as I wanted to die.

"Is there anyone you can call?" The nurse asked as she too, seemed to fight back her tears.

"Come with me. We can wait in the family room."

"I don't want to go in there. I want to see my husband," I demanded as the tears finally rolled down my cheeks.

"You can't see him now. You just can't," the nurse said as she led me to sit down. After about an hour, the doctor came in and confirmed her words.

"Mrs. Jackson, as you know there was a bad accident. It was so bad; there was nothing we could do for your husband. I'm sorry to have to tell you this."

"I want to see him," I insisted.

"We don't recommend that at this time."

"I don't care what you recommend. I want to see my husband!" I yelled as I bellowed out a strong wail of grief.

The soothing calm of my husband's voice came over me. And he told me to not come in the room; to go home and be with our children. That gave me the strength to stand up and walk out of the hospital. Without saying another word, I left and headed home to be with our children, as my husband instructed. My Mom pulled up near the entrance and took me home, she came right on time.

That night, I lay in bed alone, remembering so many conversations my husband and I shared. Just about a week ago, we were joking around with each other, and he told me when it came time for us to die, he wanted to go first because the boys needed their mother. I said, "No, you are not getting off easy like that and leaving me to suffer alone." He told me, "I mean it. I want you to take the boys and move to Fort Wayne. My parents will help you." We both became quiet and changed the subject.

With that memory, I gathered our sons and relocated to Fort Wayne. It appeared the more angry I was with God, the more He blessed me. God took such good care of me and the boys, that I was forced out of my anger. Our sons did not seem to understand in the beginning what it all meant. I just let time unfold the reality to them. Our lives were slowly coming back together, and we were headed on a road to peace. One weekend, we drove to Akron, Ohio to visit my Mom. My plans were to return Sunday to go to work at my new job as a church secretary. This particular trip, my Mom didn't want for me to leave. But keeping my commitment to the job, I did not deviate from the plans. While I was in Akron, I had a lot of detailed work done on my 1976 fire-engine red, Chevy Nova. I had new covers made for the seats, new tires, detailed cleaning and wax job, tune up and a brand new stereo with speakers. People, especially men wanted my car badly. I was not giving up my car because it reminded me of my husband. He taught me how to drive in a blue one just like it.

We made it back to Fort Wayne, Indiana. The next morning, I got up for work. The spirit was moving within me. I had not a care in the world. I felt so blessed and thankful for my life. As I drove down South Calhoun Street, one of the main streets in Fort

Wayne, I found myself interrupted from my magic moment by realizing I had my hands on the steering wheel and my foot on my brake; yet my car continued to move through the intersection at a fast rate. When I finally stopped moving, I was halted by a curb on the side of the street.

"Miss, are you all right? I tried to stop! All I could do was stay away from your gas tank!" A man wearing a flannel cut off sleeved shirt with a thick beard yelled.

I was looking at him wondering where he had come from. I did not understand his concern for me.

"Miss, I've called the police and they're on the way. Are you all right? I could have killed you! Oh my God!"

I got out of the car because people were beginning to surround us as the sounds of the sirens became near. When I looked at my car, the back end of my car was in my back seat. A truck carrying forty-tons of asphalt had reared me from the back and I never saw it coming. When the police took the report, he told me it is a miracle my car did not blow up. If I had not been driving a car with an A frame, I would not have survived. He also told me the driver was shocked, because he knew my life would have been over if he had hit my gas tank.

Three days later, I was in the hospital suffering amnesia, speech impairment, fainting spells and I could not walk straight. Loud sounds would cause me to black out. I was experiencing what they diagnosed me as with a severe whiplash and a concussion. After four months of no progress, I began to become weary. My youngest son, Marcus was not doing very well with my absence. His depression caused me to walk out of the hospital, still suffering with the same symptoms, against medical advice. My mother-in-law had to hold me to keep me from running into walls. The whiplash had thrown my vertebrae out of line.

Constantly having to take pain pills and muscle relaxers to endure the pain in my back and shoulder, confirmed the extent of my injuries. There were days I did not remember what happened. I was struggling with my new life of agony and physical pain. The wear down of doing it alone and needing my husband began creating bitterness in my heart. Six months had gone by and I was still battling the sudden loss. Many nights, I would sleep and discover I was not breathing. Waking up dizzy and weak, I would sit up all night afraid that if I fell back to sleep, I would not wake up. It was not enough to lose my husband to an accident, but now I have to live the aftermath of my own as I watched my body expand from wearing a size fourteen to twenty. The medications and inability to move transformed my body and I could not get a grip on my weight gain.

It was summer and the boys and I had no obligations to leave home. I got so depressed; I stopped answering my telephone and stopped leaving the house. By my second week, my Father-in-law came to our home. When I let him in, his face told the whole story. I was a basket case

"Lyn what are you doing? Why didn't you answer your phone?"

"I just did not want to," I said as my words slurred from the muscle relaxers.

"Willie Mae cooked supper; you and the boys come on over and eat. Get out of this house for a while."

"Alright, we're coming."

That night we had dinner with my husband's family. As I looked around the table, all I saw was his face in his Mother, Father and Sister's faces. Then, I looked at our sons and saw him there, too. I managed to hold back the tears.

That night, I got the boys to bed and prostrated my self before God. I was ashamed of my self-pity. Down on my knees, I wept. The tears I shed that night were tears not even I recognized as being my own. These tears came from deep down in my soul and filled my heart to an overflowing groaning. It was like an earthquake erupting through my being. Shaking, as I surrendered my soul to God, I prayed for forgiveness for not wanting to live anymore.

God let me know what he knew I had in my heart. I never told anyone I did not want to live anymore. But God knew it was corroding the space in my heart that belonged to him. God told me he knew my private abyss that was justifiably growing and he wanted me to know he loved me and understood my pain. He also promised me he would restore the years of the locust and my joy would be full. I cried the more in knowing God did not punish me for my bitterness.Knowing God was embracing me, Lyn, not the mother, sister or daughter this time, but I, the one who needed comfort made me want to live again.

I asked God to heal me, that I may be there for our sons. God honored my prayer and gave me strength to see Robert and Marcus grow up to be wonderful men. He restored my body and mind. Forever, I will be indebted to God, for he allowed my sons to have me in their lives. I live to be his instrument and to bless his people.   His love blesses me to be human and free. I want the world to know; He loves us dearly right where we are and there is not anything we may think, say or do, that will keep Him from loving us.   God just loves us because he is our Heavenly Father.

THE MINISTRY OF MOTHERHOOD: REFLECTIONS OF A TEENAGE MOTHER

Cheryl Lacey Donovan

Being a PK or a preacher's kid, for those not familiar with the vernacular, is not an easy thing. Somehow, when your father is called to preach, all of a sudden you're elevated to a higher standard than other children. The expectations and demands are almost unbearable at times and I spent the first fifteen years of my life doing so, as people watched in hopes of my downfall.

I was a straight A student. I participated in the student council, was secretary of the student council, and president of my sophomore class. Church participation was a given: the choir, the Baptist Training Union, and every Easter and Christmas play. I was on my way to proving the naysayer's wrong. I would not be the worst kid simply because my father was a pastor.

To my surprise, came this smooth talkin', good lookin', chocolate covered ladies man, who shook the ground beneath me. All the girls wanted him. And there was no question as to why. But, he wanted me.

Until this point, I had always done what my parents told me. No questions asked.

Persistent and patience would persevere as this young man's initial advances toward me went unanswered. I had been resilient in my efforts to resist him. Until the fateful day when my mother decided it would be okay for him to take me out. This was indeed the beginning of the end.

Being naïve in the department of male-female relationships, I was immediately smitten by his suave attitude and charming demeanor. He knew all of the right things to say. Even the very parting of his lips when he did speak had me head over heels. He spoke often of church, which lured me right in. He paid careful attention to the things that I liked to do and he showered me with gifts.

Determined not to be swayed, I held onto my convictions, for dear life, for a long time, but before long, the relationship turned into one of what I thought was true love. Needless to say, the time finally came when I was challenged to prove that love.

Don't let anyone tell you that it can't happen to you the first time. I, and my eldest son, are living witnesses that this cliché could not be further from the truth.

I was sixteen and pregnant! Not that things couldn't get any worse, unless, of course, you consider the fact that I was Preacher's Kid. Oh my God! I guess everyone was right. Preacher's kids are the worse. We always mess up.

No one would remember the straight A's or the memory verses I recited by heart. They wouldn't remember all of the sweet melodies that I sang each Sunday. They would blatantly forget the fact that I was on the fast track for graduation a year early. No…all they would save to memory is that I was a preacher's daughter; a teenager, unmarried, and pregnant. The pastor's daughter.

"How on earth would I tell my parents?" I remember thinking when the doctor told me the news. It took me almost a month before I gathered the courage to tell my mother. Even then, it was after the doctor called me to ask had I done so because I needed to start prenatal care.

My mother had been the most influential part of my life for as long as I could remember. Shaping me, molding me, and teaching me how to become a strong, independent young woman. Now, look at the mess I've made. How on earth could I be independent when I was expecting a dependent? How would I raise a child, when I was a child myself? Everyone knew that teen mothers had to go on welfare. They lived in the projects with their sorry excuses for men, duckin' and dodging the welfare workers so that the mother could keep her benefits.

How would I continue my education? Teen moms didn't finish school and neither did their offspring. Their choices were limited and their only hope was to acquire a minimum wage job at a fast food restaurant. The plan for me was to graduate high school, attend college, and get a good paying job. How was this going to happen now?

And last but not least, what of my father, the pastor? How would he live this one down? How would our family withstand the ridicule that would come our way? There's no way that the church folk would let us live this one down. After all, we had an image to uphold. How would that look? The pastor's daughter fornicated and he couldn't even control his own daughter. How can he tell us what to do? I could hear it all now. This was going to be a tough road, but there was one thing that I knew for sure. I would not have to walk it alone.

First things first. We, the young man and I, needed to make this right. The good thing was both of us had graduated from high school. As a straight A student, I had scholarships to several schools and could potentially see my way through this misfortune.

So, we did the right thing. We got married and my new husband was off to the army the next day. It was three months before I saw him again.

Eighteen, with two sons and in school was not an easy job. By this time, I had moved to another state with my new husband. I was living in housing provided by the United States Army, trying to make it work with no help and no support from the man I'd grown to cherish. The man whom I bore a son for at the tender age of sixteen.

If anyone had told me that my loving husband would find ample supplies of drugs in the army, I would have told them they were lying. But the reality of the situation was, the first family meeting that we had on base talked about the abundance of drugs on the base. In fact, a captain had been dishonorably discharged for growing marijuana right there on the base.

It wasn't long before the drugs that were so readily available on the base came home to roost. My husband began using and I became his punching bag. Determined that he would never hit me again, I devised a plan to go back to our hometown with him to pick up a car that his mother had bought. I knew that once I got back to my family, I would never go back with him. So, I began packing all that I could. This was not going to be easy, as the recent years of my life had proven to be as I was responsible to two sons, after giving birth to my second child, only sixteen months after the first was born.

Once we arrived in our home city, I moved in with my mother. I told my husband that I was moving in with my mother and would not be going back. His pleas were pointless and I had made up my mind. Even at that young age, my mother instilled in me that I was never to be anyone's punching bag. He had to return or be considered AWOL.

Here I was again caught in a situation that could have meant my demise. I was a young single mother who had not yet completed a post secondary degree. And I was back living with my mother.

Of course my husband, feeling dejected by my untimely departure, was dead set on not providing support for the children. Once he found out that the army would automatically send me money, he made certain that he was discharged. How he was able to stay under the radar for so many years, I will never know, but the battle for support went on for years. You know, the Attorney General seemed to only care about children receiving support from the non-custodial parent when the custodial parent is on welfare. When all attempts failed through the government, I tried to go through private companies to get some help. Their only response was, "Ma'am, everyone is trying to get money from him." He married again and eventually had four other children.

Getting public assistance was not any better. The Department of Human Services told me that my parents made too much money; therefore, I could not get anything from the government while I stayed in the same house with my parents.

"So, now what Lord?" I questioned.

His answer, "Trust in me with all your heart and lean not to your own understanding. In all your ways acknowledge me and I will direct your path."

In retrospect, I now understand that all of this was God's plan, and part of it was to teach me how to trust only in Him.

My children didn't need their father in their life at the time. He was on drugs, he was an abuser, and in general, he had no real direction in his life. So, from that point on, I chose not to pursue money from him. This way I knew that I would never be challenged about visitation. Making this decision, however, meant that I would now have to fast forward my plan so that I could take care of the boys alone.

My mother was extremely instrumental in making this happen. She supported me emotionally, physically, and even financially until I could get on my feet. She ministered to me in ways no one else could. She led by example. She showed me that no matted how deep the mess was, a mother's love would reach down and pull you out.

Fast forward twenty-four years. My oldest son was now a college graduate and teaching computer technology in the local school district. My youngest son was nearing the completion of his college degree. I was happily married to my second husband of fourteen years and I became an author, mentor, and educator.

I was never on welfare and both of my children went to school with academic scholarships.

Raising two sons was not an easy task. God placed many people in my life to help me make my transition. How did I do it? I sought the Lord and he answered me. He told me in his word that I could do all things through Christ who strengthens me. He said that a good woman, a worthy woman was worth more than rubies and that is what I wanted to be. He said that he would do exceedingly and abundantly more than I could ever ask Him for. He said in his word, that if I made myself at home with Him, and made His words a home in me, that I could be sure that whatever I asked, would be listened to and acted upon. God became my ultimate source. He did not give me a spirit of fear, but of love, power and a sound mind. I became like Paul, it mattered very little to me what others thought of me, or my situation, because only God could judge. As a result, I could now stand firmly and testify to the fact that God is faithful, and that He will honor His word.

My journey was intensely rough, and the challenge of rising to the top, made me want to crumble at times, but the footprints in the sand were not my own. I had to make a commitment to God, to myself, and to my children. This was the only way that we could make it to where we are now.

This meant working, getting an education and being available to my children at all costs. Trivial pursuits like partying and staying out all night would have to be placed on the backburner. I was on a mission. The mission of being a virtuous woman, of being a dedicated mother. I wanted to be worth more than rubies.

I could remember all the financial difficulties I encountered during my journey. Although I was making more than the minimum wage, so that in and of itself was a blessing. But, I can also remember many times when the lights had to go, or the water had to go, or even the phone, but God was so faithful, he always had a ram in the bush and the distress was only for a moment. Tthere were many times that I just wanted to give up and throw in the towel; when it seemed that there was no light at the end of the tunnel. Days when the bills seemed to outnumber the income were the same days when that little voice inside would remind me that God was still in control. He would not let me come to a point and then just leave me.

Staying true to my original plan would've broken some of the strongest of women. I worked tirelessly in the medical field until I made it to a point in the profession where I now teach other medical students. I led by example to show my sons that a good work ethic was important especially for African American males in the South.

Frequent visits to my son's school, attending church on a regular basis, and plenty of activities for the boys occupied much of my time. The result were truly rewarding. When I see children that grew up before, during and after my boys on the street corners, in gangs, strung out on drugs, in jail, or dead breaks my heart. Many people have ridiculed, laughed at, and otherwise mocked my tactics for childrearing because I respected my children and I listened to them so that I could transition them from parent controlled behavior to self controlled behavior. I nurtured their gifts and spoke good things into their lives.

The triumph of my soul rested in knowing that I took the ministry of motherhood seriously. I was blessed with the knowledge that my love was the closest thing to God's love on this side of Heaven. It was unconditional, forgiving, and unmotivated. As a result, my children have experienced the favor of God in many ways.

The Bible said that we should honor our father and our mother so that our days may be long upon the earth. It did not say that we should do this only when our parents do the right things. In my ministry as a mother, I asked the Lord to teach me how to forgive, truly, and how to teach my children to love their father in spite of his shortcomings.

God also taught me to love again, to feel again. My soul was set free from the hatred that I felt towards a man that had hurt me deeply, the guilt that I felt for disappointing my parents, and the self loathing I felt for letting myself down in the beginning. God replaced my disparaging thoughts with feelings of hope, faith, and victory.

Seeing the father of my children confirmed what I knew God had done for me. He made my soul free and at peace. I was able to accept his apology in the spirit in which it was given and move on with no expectations and no regrets. Learning to forgive was truly a triumph of my soul, because once that happened, I was able to let true love in and soar to a place that no one could touch.

God opened my heart and mind and allowed me to love. Someone very special came into my life and provided a love so strong that no one could take it away. Glory be to God, that my husband, the man God sent my way, was able to provide my sons, as best he could, with the tools necessary for them to become good men.

His love for God is an attribute and he displays it boldly before all who would see. He taught me how to love again; how to trust again, and how to live again. He was patient, he was kind, and he was definitely longsuffering. It was these fruits of the spirit that let me know that he was truly a Godsend.

Yes, my soul triumphed over adversity, and I prayed that through my vocation, I would be able to help others in their quest for a triumphant life in God.

BREAKING THE CHAINS OF ABUSE

Cascheé Russell

Are you sure you want to do this?" Raynard, the love of my life, asked.

I squeezed his protective hand tightly. "I'm ready." My palms were sweaty and I was swinging my left leg back and forth as it dangled across my right one.

Although I feared public speaking, I knew I had to tell my story. Facing an auditorium filled with women and children who were abuse victims, like myself, would serve as a heavy responsibility. We were here to tell our stories and pray that not another person would suffer the abuse that we experienced from our tormentors. I was well equipped to testify how God saved me from the personal hell that Darian Wright put me through. I refused to be a victim, and with the strength He gave me, I would prevent every soul I could touch, from being a victim, too. If I had my way, this day would mark the end for abuse forever.

Mrs. Maria Divine, the director of the "Real Love Doesn't Break Bones and Bleed program, announced me as the next guest speaker to share my personal experience with domestic abuse. I walked up the stairs, strong and confident, with a Dannon water bottle and my convictions behind me. I fought to keep my composure, positioning the microphone closer to my trembling lips. I looked out into the crowd. Raynard gave me two thumbs up and a confident smile. That gave me the courage to share my pain with the women before me.

I took another deep breath and wiped the tears of strength away from my eyes. I was mentally and emotionally prepared to convey my personal testimony to the ladies at the Safe Haven for Battered Women and Children.

"Good afternoon." The women returned my greeting in unison. "I was raised on

the Eastside of Detroit. My name is Monae Brown, and just like you ladies in attendance, I am also a survivor. My abuser was four years older than me. His name was Darian Wright. He was a liar, a cheater, and a very negative person who abused alcohol and drugs."

"I met Darian one day when I was riding my bike. He was trying to flirt with me. I purposely ignored him until he smiled. That was the only nice thing about him." A few of the women giggled at my remark. Even I was able to smile as my body relaxed. "Darian and I were from two very different sides of the train tracks. He was a high school dropout and I was an honor student who worked on the high school newspaper. I was lonely, and the attention he gave me made him attractive, so I gave him my time. He resembled old school rapper, Big Daddy Kane. It was too bad for me that I was a huge Big Daddy Kane fan." More giggles came from the women as I felt a connection with my audience.

"That's one of the main reasons I took his telephone number and called him. One week later, we went to the AMC theatre to see "I'm Gonna get You Sucka" with Keenan Ivory Wayans. Afterwards, we went to the all-you-can-eat-buffet at Big Boy's restaurant. He had money. I foolishly thought that money and his love would change my life. And it did so, but not the way that a young girl like me would have hoped for. My choice to date him was wrong on so many levels." The tears I tried my best to hold back came rushing forward. The most painful part of my testimony was about to be told. Inhaling, then exhaling, I regained my composure and continued.

"Darian physically assaulted me when I was nine months pregnant with our twins. He attacked me with his fists and his feet. I didn't even remember what brought on the attack. His mother sent me away from their home in a cab. I was bloody and bruised. My body was broken and my spirit was devastated. I was having severe pains in my stomach. The driver rushed me to the hospital after my water broke in the back seat of the dirty car. Alexus, my daughter, was born healthy. My son, Alex, was born fifteen minutes later in critical condition with a cracked skull, broken fingers, and a broken rib cage. He died three hours later as a result of Darian's violent abuse. If Alex had survived, there would have been brain damage so severe that he would have never enjoyed a normal life."

I could see other women in the audience shedding tears as I relived the pain of losing my son. My voice trembled as I continued speaking. "That memory still saturates my heart and soul. Profound grief consumes me when I think about how I was robbed of watching him become all that I knew he could have been. His laughter, I miss terribly, even though I've never heard it. That memory alone shakes my soul to the core. But my heart smiles at the end of the night because I know he's watching me from Heaven." I said, looking upward at the ceiling. Alex was there in heaven watching over his family.

"It's unbelievable that I'm still alive to share my story of survival. God is good and He has shown me time and time again that He has bigger plans for me. I would love to say that the death of my son marked the end of my nightmare with Darian, but it didn't. I didn't the strength to walk away. I was weak for him. I thought I needed his love. And I thought my love could change him. I was wrong, but oddly, I don't regret it. into, because had that been the end between us, I wouldn't have had my baby daughter, Corvette. No matter what I went through with Darian Wright, I love my daughters and I thank God for them every single day of my life."

"And there was his mother. Mrs. Wright was a witness to my personal pain several times. Most of the time during the attacks, she would just close her bedroom door and turn her radio up, so she could drown out my screams. How could a mother allow her son to abuse another woman's child? Was it because she too had been a victim of abuse? Had she been his abuser? I don't know just where the chain of abuse began with Darian and his family. I just know that there are so many excruciating memories of what Darian has done to me and the memories still make my soul scream and holler for spiritual relief. My painful experience broke me down, but God gave me the strength to remain motivated and to move forward."

I sipped my water and said a heartfelt prayer to continue my testimony. "Sometimes it was hard not to hate both Darian and his mother. But hate is not how we overcome pain. Hate only nurtures pain. Only with love can we truly let go of all the hatred and heal. Only with God's love can we truly forgive and feel free. I prayed for women like Mrs. Wright. She, too, needed strength because no mother closes her eyes and heart when she sees her son abusing a woman. The pain and anger I felt towards his mother inspired the words to my poem *What Are You Doing, My Sister?*"

Tears flowed from my eyes while I recited my verses.

Where's the get up and go My Sister?

What are you Pursuing?

Time waits on No one.

So tell me, what are you doing?

Make plans to secure your future before another day,

Turns into night and runs away to sway,

Persevere and don't allow Low self esteem to Win,

It has in the past because of what you've seen and where you've been,

What are you doing My Sister distributing attitudes unable to fold,

Is your personality Sweet, Understanding, Revengeful or Cold,

And to my Spiritual sister's, Glory be to God,

Without our Heavenly Father's guidance, love and mercy, we will all be lost and robbed,

What are you doing my Sister are you trying to make things right?

Or are you a Down for whatever Chick that's eager to get arrested tonight,

What are you doing, My Sister? Are you being a Good Mother to your child,

Or are you Ignoring them to party like rock stars at the clubs, while your precious child is running wild,

My Sister why are you still in that abusive relationship?

Bruises doesn't Lie, So stop trying to hide that Black eye and Busted Lip,

Calm down My Sister, Respect yourself sexually instead of getting all stressed out,

    Enduring Unhealthy Drama and Jealousy is what You Can live without,

What are you doing my Sister? Are you jumping in and out of all these Strange Men beds to receive long awaited attention,

Please stop Disrespecting your Body just for a two minute plunge of fabricated affection,

And to My little Sisters, enjoy your childhood,

Because doing any and everything to please others is not all good,

Do you really think, You need a Man to be Successful, Is that why you're singing the Blues?

Wake up, My Sisters because Confidence and Determination is priceless, Listen If Your Man can make it in Big Business, then You can too,

What are you doing my sister, Are you allowing the Lies from Hate and Racism to Destroy you,

*Listen, Race doesn't define who you are or who you will
become, Perseverance does! So go after the Career you want to
Pursue,*
*My Sisters, why are you Starving yourself because the Barbie's
say Skinny is in,*
*Well you're wrong, because Beauty comes in all sizes and You
can be Sexy and Thick without being sickly and thin,*
*My Sister's of all colors, Embrace this Reality inspired Thunder
in this Poetic Storm and Rise,*
*Straight to the Top with Passion in your Heart, Confidence in
your Actions, and Commitment in your eyes,*
*Please Wake Up my Beautiful, and Talented Sister's, and
become a Woman on the Move! because your Life is Calling,*
So what are you pursuing?
*Please answer with Authority My Sister's So everyone will
know what you think, how you feel and What you're doing?*

The poem brought more tears to my eyes. When I finished,
one of the women in the audience stood up and shouted, "Take
your time, Baby! It's all right! You're a survivor! And most of
all, he'll never hurt you again."

"Thank you. The last time I was attacked by Darian was on
Mother's Day, of all days. He invited us over for breakfast. As
soon as I walked into their house, he gave me a broken red rose
and an inflated Mother's Day balloon. That should have been
the first red flag. Darian never gave me anything. His little act
didn't last long. He disappeared into the bathroom after breakfast.
My youngest daughter had fallen asleep. She was resting
comfortably in her grandmother's bed. Alexus, my oldest, was

out back with her grandmother. I was left in the dining room with Darian's younger brother. He had a new CD player and asked if I wanted to listen to Queen Latifah's *U.N.I.T.Y.* I placed the headphones over my ears and watched him disappear out the front door. No sooner than he left did I feel cold metal around my neck. Darian was choking me with the fifteen-inch dog chain that he used to intimidate his pit bull. I was gasping for air and kicking my feet wildly. He pulled harder and harder. I couldn't breathe and I knew that I had to do something if I was going to leave that house alive. I prayed and God granted me strength to reach up and grab hold to a handful of Darian's braided hair. 'Bitch!' he yelled as he stumbled back. I dropped the twisted hair from my hands. His scalp was bleeding. He rushed towards the bathroom and I kicked off my flip-flops and ran out the front door! I didn't want to leave my children behind. I wanted to grab the both of them, but I didn't know how much time I had before he came chasing behind me. His mother was in the backyard with Alexus, and in my heart, I knew she would take care of my daughters until my mother and I returned to pick them up. I ran as fast as I could for my life. Before I was even half way down the street I heard a loud gun shot. My heart felt like it was about to jump out of my chest. I turned around, almost frozen in fear, because the gunshots were being fired at me. It was Darian running down the street and shooting at me! He had always made verbal threats about shooting me with one of his guns. I just didn't think he would actually do it in broad daylight with a street full of people standing around as witnesses. But he didn't care who was watching. Besides the criminals who did their dirt in his neighborhood were not snitches. No one would care if he shot and killed me.

The reality of Darian killing me gave me an adrenaline rush as I pumped my arms and ran as fast as I could. I ran track back at Finney High School and I remembered zigzag runs, one of our track drills. I moved side to side as he continued to shoot at me! I knew my Heavenly father was going to deliver me from death's door. I wasn't shot, but I was knocked down by a speeding car. I still have severe back problems to this day from being hit. The driver got me away from Darian. My guardian angel, my Alex, was there with me. My life was spared because I needed to be here. I needed to be here to share with all of you. I thank God and His son Jesus Christ every day I wasn't silenced by Darian's gun." I looked out into the crowd and saw women of all ages and color who had been in my shoes. Some were still in those shoes.

I received a standing ovation for my testimony. There wasn't a dry eye in the building, including mine. Feeling accomplished, I turned away from the microphone and walked down the stairs to take my seat. But to my surprise, all of the ladies at the Safe Haven, chanted for an encore.

I walked eagerly back up the stairs and back over toward the mic "Ladies, I would like to thank you so much for the love. As strange as it sounds, I thank Darian. I thank Darian for being who he was. Had I not met him, and gone through so much pain, I wouldn't know how to appreciate the loving man God has blessed me with." I pointed towards Raynard and smiled. "I love you so much. Thank you for giving my girls and I what we needed most. Thank you for bringing God into our hearts, Raynard. Thank you for loving us."

Everyone clapped thunderously as I returned to my seat to join Raynard.

"Can I escort you to dinner, my lady?" he asked as we left the Safe Haven and walked slowly towards my Ford Expedition.

"Dinner? What do you have in mind?" I smiled at him lovingly.

He pampered me and showered me with so much love and affection. Before him I was lost in a world of depression. There was no waking up on Sunday morning taking my kids and myself to church. We had no way to get there and I truly had no desire to be there. But then Raynard, a man of God, came along. He reintroduced me to Christ and the beauty within.

"Well, Mom has the girls, so the night is ours." Raynard replied, twinkling his eyes. I knew he was up to something, but I couldn't imagine what.

"Red Lobster?" I asked. It was my favorite restaurant and Raynard agreed. We pulled out of the parking lot and headed towards Red Lobster listening to my favorite CD, *The Best of Whitney Houston.*

Raynard parked right in front of the building when we arrived at our destination. I sat patiently and waited for him to open my door as he had always done. He escorted me inside the restaurant with a strong arm around my waist. I felt so safe in his arms.

During our dinner, I excused myself to the restroom. I was enjoying the food, the relaxing atmosphere, and of course, Raynard's company. I returned to find candles lit and roses spread across our table.

"What's going on, Baby?" I asked as my heart skipped a beat. From somewhere I heard music playing. It was Brian McKnight's soulful voice.

"Raynard?" Tears filled my eyes as I looked down at him. He had answered my first question by dropping down on one knee. He then pulled a ring box from his pants pocket. When he opened it, I was nearly blinded by the one-carat diamond!

"Monae, I love you with all my heart. You're the strongest woman I've ever met and I want nothing more than to have you as my wife. Let me be a father to your girls. Let me be your husband. Will you marry me?"

"Yes!" I screamed. "Yes! I'll marry you!" There was no way I could say no. Raynard embraced my ready-made family. He didn't run from the responsibility of fatherhood. My girls were not his by birth, but he was willing to be the father to them that Darian wasn't man enough to be. I didn't know who was happier. Raynard scooped me up in his strong arms after placing the rock on my finger. He kissed me lovingly and passionately. We both cried tears of joy as the people around us clapped and cheered.

My life went from hell to heaven. It was because I found God again. He gave me the strength to trust and to love once more. Without Him, I never would have been able to find the true love I found in my husband, Raynard. I was happy to say that we now have four beautiful kids. We had three daughters and one son at home. And we would never forget about our son, Alex, up in heaven. He was our guardian angel.

WHEN YOU LEAST EXPECT
Dike Okoro

Help me Lord," I heard myself uttering, "Help me get out of this forest of pain and regrets. I've fought the battle alone, and time has not been kind to me. Yet my spirit refuses to succumb to the memories mocking my silence."

Shadows of my past have turned me into a believer in half-truths. In the company of friends and people I know, I imagine and ponder what they think of me. Like the night breaks its silence to condemn the desires of lovers, I reach into my inner thoughts daily, to dig deep and search for the burning candle threatened by the fears that plague my past. My group meetings and counseling sessions in church have only helped to delay the wrath of the nightmares I have tried so desperately to run away from.

Each day I stand in front of the mirror and slap and rub cream on my cheek and brush my hair to my satisfaction. I have fed my heart to those words I have not been courageous enough to disclose to Safisha. How do I tell my fiancé and best friend of three years that I am jobless, with our wedding date only two months away?

When You Least Expect

Many a time, I have sat in bed in the condo overlooking the lake on Sheridan Road, alone, fumbling through the classified job section of the *Chicago Tribune* and the *Chicago Sun Times*, seeking possibilities in the flooded and yet convoluted job market. Twice in one month I have been to Pastor Wright's counseling sessions. And twice I have gone home buried in disappointment. "Brother, you've got to keep the faith. But you must first seek God's guidance in prayers," I recall the ever modest Pastor telling me. In truth, he was right. The doors to the hole I have suddenly found myself can only be opened by me. But I have to get rid of my fears, and I have to work a little bit harder to get what I want.

Safisha knew about my predicament. Yet she would wake up in the morning and make the best breakfast in the world. Fried eggs. Bacon, and French toast. We ate on time and left home on time. Safisha worked at the bookstore at Chicago State University as a cashier. I don't know how we made it or barely survived on the meager salary she made. But we fared well all right. Sometimes I looked at her with disdain, or maybe it was jealousy. I had a master's degree in psychology from Northeastern Illinois University, Chicago. Why I studied for a degree in such an area of study remained a mystery to me. Yet I could recall how much I enjoyed the challenge of campus life; the exams, the friends. And not to forget the professors who made it all happen with their persistence and support to guide and shape students. I did the best I could to get out in four years. Those were the hardest years of my life. I caught the early train, six-thirty in the morning, to be specific, to Wilson Avenue. And then I waited on the bus to the university's gate. The harsh winter did not stop, especially since I didn't have a car to depend on.

My father owned a computer business in Boston and had always wanted me to join him once I was through with school. But pride won't let me embrace the reason behind his motive. Not even when Safisha tried to talk me into accepting my father's offer and we ended up containing ourselves through a harangue. I wanted things my way.

I wanted to make things happen for Safisha and myself through our efforts, without the interference or what I had considered my parents babysitting approach to support me.

Yes, I had finally arrived at the crossroad. No job, armed with a master's degree, but selling watermelon on 95th and King Drive to raise rent and food money in the condo I shared with Safisha. I would pull my baseball cap down low to cover my face and watch the scorching sun of summer rise until it faded at about seven in the evening. The grinding protest of tires and the blast of car horns kept me awake through the day. And when it was time to leave, Mr. Bradford gave me a watermelon to take home. I thanked him then and left right away. I had to hurry home on the red line so I could get some rest before catching the brown line at night to work at the UPS on Broadway and Clark Avenue.

Yet July was a terrible month for me. The pain I experienced when I came home at about seven in the morning to have a shower and get ready for my job as a watermelon seller, was excruciating. "Baby, it's going to be okay," Safisha would say, looking at herself in the mirror while applying make up. "The

Lord will provide." What did I know of my slowly fading faith in the Lord? What did I reckon of the blessings of going to sleep for four hours, from eight in the morning to twelve noon, just so I could have some fresh legs to depend on while standing in the sun on King Drive? "Yeah, where has the Lord been all this while, with my impressive resume and job applications to the city colleges ignored and probably considered worthless, eh?" Safisha would look at me and then gather her handbag and books and leave, after a sharing a quick kiss.

I resented the idea of positivism in those days. "Don't panic, men," I would say to myself. And when my mom called me to know how we were faring, I always told her everything was all right. I would listen to everything she had to say about dad, the house, the car, the dog, and church. "Did you and Safisha arrange to meet with the good reverend?" she would ask. And I always had the right answer. My yes was always taken for a signal that I did not want to stay on the phone. Poor mom; she hung up after then. And in my silence, I would suffer the decadence of my yearning to be left alone.

Although my strategy worked, I would later learn that I was doing myself more harm than good. My patience was running out. The car notes, the car insurance payment, the credit cards bills, and the rent had to be paid. What did I know of living a life with money in demand at all times? I had finally begun to feel the pressure of the heat. And that was when I started taking dad's suggestions seriously. I recall waking up one morning and saying to myself, "To hell with UPS and the watermelon job." Jesus! Damn the jobs. I used to laugh at myself those days. A black male with a graduate degree in America, yet a watermelon seller? Not to think of the fact that I have never been to the jail or even been arrested. Shocking. No kidding. I could have easily settled with flipping burgers at McDonald's or Burger King. But my priorities had changed after I walked that stage to collect my second diploma. Such thoughts crossed my mind until that morning I called Safisha on the phone and told her I was catching the Greyhound Bus to Boston.

It was one of those sunny, but windy days in Chicago. I came downstairs and the streets were crowded with faces, and the traffic jam was extreme. By the time I got to the train station and caught the red line and got off at Jackson station to catch the Greyhound Bus, I had already made up my mind never to return to my jobs, ever.

Safisha did not call back after I told her I was on my way to Boston. But I was not bothered. I knew why she was upset. That was her way of protesting the fact that I always took decisions and then consulted her afterwards. But I had to do what I had to do. With our wedding already scheduled for September, I had to look for a way to raise money. It wasn't about me anymore. I had suddenly realized there was more to things I had taken for granted for the past three months.

When I got to my parents mansion in Boston, it was already ten o'clock at night, and I was completely tired from the fifteen hours or so trip. I went to the kitchen and fixed myself a plate of macaroni and cheese. Then I took a bottle of water from the refrigerator and went to the living room. Sports Center was airing on ESPN. I sat in front of the television and started devouring my repast when Safisha called. "Hey baby," she started. "How was your trip?" I took a second to swallow the food in my mouth and then guzzle the glass of water, before saying, "All right." We talked briefly, and then I assured Safisha I was going to call her later that night. But sleep took over me. The penalty for eating so late I guess.

The next morning I had a lengthy conversation with dad before he left for work. "Sit down son," he started. Dressed in a black suit and red tie, with his grey moustache and beard proclaiming his age, dad sat down and waited for me to speak. Mom listened, although she was still having her breakfast. I let dad know how I felt about working for him like he had always wanted. "But I know you came to visit for another reason son.

What is it? I have got work to do in the office." I looked him in the eyes and finally told him I was looking for a job. "You've always loved teaching since your freshman year in college. Did you apply for a teaching position?" Dad asked. I was not at all at ease with his question. I came because I wanted him to support me with money, or at least loan me some money I could repay. But I knew Dad well enough. He would make me work for my money, rather me than loan money to me. After pondering for a second, he told me to call him in the office at about nine, that he had an idea he would like to share with me.

That evening dad gave me a check for ten thousand dollars. He didn't ask me to repay him. All he told me was that I had to use the money reasonably until I got a job. Weighed down by a heavy heart, I wept while hugging and thanking him. "It's okay son. You be good now. Just do as I say, okay," Dad said. I

looked at the check again, in disbelief of what had happened. I
called Pastor Wright and told him all that had happened. "Son,
you've got to believe the Lord," he said. "See you in church next
Sunday." I got off the phone and called Safisha. I did not tell her
about the money, but I told her my parents had gifted us some
money.

It was dark outside when I gathered my belongings and
informed Dad and Mom I was on my way to the Greyhound Bus
station on Saint James Avenue to catch a Chicago- bound bus.
After they dropped me off at the station, I watched Dad's Range
Rover crawl 'til it picked up speed and disappeared in traffic. The
night sky was full of stars. The moon peered honorably. There
were assorted vehicles firing down opposite ends on the free
way. Now and then, some detail of what to do with the money
seeped out of my mind. But I had to get to Chicago first. Earlier
in the day, I had pleaded with Dad to cash the money. And he
had done so to my satisfaction. I had little need to be worried. I
separated the money and put half in a plastic bag in my suitcase.
The other half I had in my jeans pocket.

When we arrived at the Chicago station of the Greyhound
Bus line on West Harrison Avenue, it was about twelve in the
morning that Saturday. I called Safisha and told her I was in
town. Then I hurried down the street toward the blue line. I had
to make a quick connection to the red line so I could get home
on time. I saw two men dressed in tatters smoking reefah and
drinking liquor. They were the only people waiting on the train
when I got down to the railroad stands. "You better hurry back
upstairs," I said to myself. But I had to get home that night.

Besides, I wanted to surprise Safisha. A train traveling express rocketed past, and within a split second, one of the men snatched my bag, and the other pushed me against the wall. By the time I regained composure and stood up, both men were gone. My bag, however, was on the ground, but they had taken the five thousand. Yes, I knew that because the plastic in which I put the money was missing. Shaking, I looked here and there to make sure both men were completely out of sight. And then I took the escalator back upstairs to report the incident to the station attendant. "Calm down. Are you okay? You need me to call the police?" the lady asked. I nodded.

Within ten minutes two police officers, a man and woman had shown up. They escorted me to the streets and began their series of questions. The streetlights flashed from every corner. The squad cars soon increased. "Sir, we need you to describe both men," the male officer said. I was still a bit jittery, for I had not fully recovered from the shove that sent me to the ground. I told him a white male and a black male were responsible for the attack. They took more notes based on questions they deemed relevant. Then they asked me if I needed a ride home or to the nearest train station. By this time my heart had stopped beating heavily.

I finally caught the red line at Jackson after being dropped off by both officers and got off at Morse Avenue at about one-fifty a.m. that morning. Safisha was still watching television when I came home. I did not tell her what I had been through hours ago. Instead I went straight to the bathroom and had a cold shower. Then I went straight to bed. Five minutes later, she came to the room. "Baby, is something the matter?" she asked. I looked at her and chuckled. Then I held her hand and pulled her close to me. She chuckled. Then we both looked each other in the eye. "I am fine," I said. "Just a bit tired. That's all." We stayed that way 'til we both fell asleep.

In the morning, we woke up and started getting ready for the day. Safisha had already woken up earlier to take her shower and get dressed. She was now eating breakfast when I got to the living room. I returned to the bathroom to wash my face and brush my teeth. "You know baby, there's this man who has been calling and asking after you," Safisha said. I didn't get what she meant at first. After all, I have only been away for about three days. So I sat next to her and took a slice of bread. "And what does he want?" I asked. She shrugged, and then handed me the jelly. I scooped a little potion and rubbed it on my bread. "Said to call him. I think he said they already sent you a letter," Safisha concluded.

I was not interested in whoever had called while I was away. I had just escaped what could have been a fatal attack last night. And the last thing on my mind was any telephone call from a telemarketer. So I calmly finished my breakfast and sat on the sofa. Safisha asked me about my parents and how they were both faring. She also asked if I had heard from Pastor Wright. We were still talking when I gathered my mail from the table next to the sofa.

Safisha sat next to me and was looking at the mail I had opened when the phone rang. She picked it up. "Yes, this is his residence," she answered. The officers who had asked me questions last night after the attack at the railway had two suspects in their custody and wanted me to come to the station to identify both men. When Safisha handed the phone over to me and watched me hang up after talking, she was curious. "Baby, what is going on? Why are you talking to the police?" I calmed her down and explained all that happened at the train station. Without consulting with me, she called in at work that morning and offered to go with me to the police station. I was elated. "Such good show of support from a woman who cared for you and loved you," I said to myself. By the time I went in and got dressed and came back to the living room, there was someone on the phone asking for me. This time it was a social service worker from the Belmont area. She asked me if I was still interested in a job I applied for with her organization since January. How do I explain that? I applied for a job and never heard from the people running the search for almost eight months. And here I was and they are asking me if I was still interested in the job. "Yes, madam, I am still interested in the job," I told the woman right away.

"Good. We're glad to know that you are still interested in working for us and are offering you the position as a social service worker. We'll discuss the benefits with you when you come in to fill out and sign some papers. Can you come in today?"

"Yes, yes!"

"Good. Why don't I give you our address information then."

My insides warmed with joy. A flowering of excitement unfolded inside my stomach. Safisha hugged me. We both wept.

Dike Okoro

With our wedding only two months away, we were beginning to see the signs of that day becoming a blessed reality. We both hurried to leave the house and head straight for the police station downtown and for the social work place at Belmont. But before we left, we called Pastor Wright to share the good news with him. "Told ya, told ya! The Lord has his own time, but you gotta believe," he said.

And what more could I had done or said to celebrate the blessing such a day had brought upon us. All I knew was that things had suddenly changed for the better. Yes, I felt it in my bones, I saw it in Safisha's eyes, and in the sun recoiling into the skies as we walked the streets to catch the train that morning.

DOORS
Ebonee Monique

I didn't like doors. I didn't like the sound they make when they open. I didn't like the uncertainty I felt when I knocked on one and I definitely didn't like the sound of them closing. That's why when I bought my first house, I took the door off of every hinge, out of every doorway. Well, except the front door, of course, I left that one alone. I stood silent, in one of the bare doorways, with my hands on my hips. I curled my fingers deep into my skin. I wasn't this upset since Rodney King got beat down and I couldn't remember how long ago that was.

"Where are you going?" I asked as I watched him pack his clothes neatly in his Nike gym bag. I could feel my blood boiling as I sucked my teeth and posed the question again. This time, though, I wasn't as refined. "I know you hear me! I said where are you going?"

He looked over his shoulder and shook his head. I plopped on the bed and watched him pack slowly. My eyes met with his hands, those strong masculine hands that had so many of our memories embedded in them. I closed my eyes and reached out to him, only to feel his arm snatching back from me.

"What'd I do to you?" I questioned, shooting my eyes open.

Sure we'd fought the night before, but I knew our love making session immediately afterwards was just the right amount of medicine to cure any animosity he harbored.

I wasn't really sure how I'd gotten here. I was thirty-two, fairly attractive, physically fit, and a 4th grade teacher in Los Angeles. I owned my own home and car and I was in love with *him*.

I call him *him* because that was all he was. He made it clear that he wasn't *the one*, *my honey* or even *my boo*. He told me plainly in my ear one night, as we made love, that he wasn't going to get hooked on me and that this was only a short-term thing. That was three years, four months and three days ago.

My ears heard the words he spoke, but my heart, soul and body had a mind of their own. I tried to tell them not to get captivated by his long flowing dread-locks, deliciously smooth dark chocolate skin and stunning jet black eyes, but they did. They throbbed, ached, and most of all, they loved him. They would've done any and everything to make him see that I was *the one*.

Like the time I traveled to Orlando cross country by car just to hear his band playing at the House of Blues. Or the time I colored my hair the exact color of his ex-girlfriend's hair because he loved it so much. When he told me he didn't like women who went out dancing, I stopped. *I was too old anyway*, that was what I told myself. And when he demanded I give up my Sundays in order to travel with him and his band, I didn't flinch. Sure, I missed church but this was what God sent me, right? I needed to make any and every sacrifice to hold onto him. I needed to be exactly who he wanted me to be. I had to make him see, what he obviously already hadn't, I was *the one*.

He swept past me barely grazing my shoulder and I tailed him. He was headed towards the front door. My short legs struggled to keep up with him, but I reached him. I tugged at his arm and he spun around to me with a look of hatred, anger and disgust plastered all over his face.

"Where are you going?" I asked again, this time with a nervous quiver in my voice.

He scanned me from the bottom of my feet to the top of my head.

"I'm leaving," he answered, gripping his bag straps on his shoulder.

"Leaving? Why?"

"I can't take you anymore and I've found someone else."

He said this before, but somehow landed right back in my life. I stood in front of the door, smacked my teeth and smiled as I approached him. I ran my hand up and down his chest and cooed, "I'll do whatever you want me to do." It was a line I said from the day our bodies first intertwined and I lived by in our relationship. His eyes followed my hand down his chest like he was trying to make a decision. He removed my hand from his body and screamed at the top of his lungs.

"I told you I didn't love you and I told you this wasn't forever!" he yelled in one breath. His beautiful jet black eyes were now bulging out of his skull. "You're spineless, needy and too clingy and I can't take it anymore!"

My eyes welled up with tears. "But I did everything you—"

"Exactly," he interrupted as his dreadlocks fell in his face, "but do you even know who *you* are?"

I stood silent trying to understand the words coming out of his mouth. Confusion consumed me whole as my heart felt like it was done pumping and my blood stopped flowing. I felt a wave of heat come over my face as I struggled for something to say. Memories flashed in front of my face of all the times my friends and family members had told me to get my priorities straight.

"You need to get back in church, girl," my sassy friend Cassandra said over lunch one day.

"You're better off by yourself if you're going to deal with that." Faith, my eclectic girlfriend from high school, said sitting across from us.

"He'll come around." I said, blowing all of them off with certainty. But in the pit of my stomach I always knew coming around would never be. I ignored the red flags God threw up so many times when everyone I knew and loved began distancing themselves from me. I still could only see him as the one I could run to.

I stood in the living room staring into his eyes for an ounce of sympathy and compassion. The hot tears streamed down my face. My bottom lip trembled along with my hands. I was struggling to keep myself together.

"Are you done, yet?" he asked coldly with his hand on the

door knob. He was ready to go before I was ready to let him go.

I heard it said so many times before that love was blind because I felt this was love. I couldn't let go of the many times he made me laugh or we cried together. I couldn't walk away from all the memories. If he left, he wasn't just leaving me, he was leaving us and I couldn't bear the thought.

I frantically rushed towards him, as he approached the door, wrapped my arms around his body and kissed him passionately.

"Maybe if I love him right, he'll stay," I thought, forcing my tongue into his mouth. He struggled to pull me off of him, but I was a force to be reckoned with.

"Get off of me!" he yelled, tearing me off of his face. I stumbled backwards and swiftly caught my balance against a wall.

"Please don't leave me!" I begged pathetically.

If I was watching this on television, I probably would have yelled at the girl to get her dumb self together and kick that loser out. But I couldn't because the dummy was me.

"Look at yourself, Carmen," he said, sounding concerned and annoyed at the same time.

Leaning against the wall, I reached out to him. He nodded his head and pulled at the door knob. My body shook ferociously upon hearing the creak of my front door opening. He was leaving. I watched his back as he slowly walks out of the door before slamming it. I slid down the wall and sat on the floor waiting for him to return. I sat motionless for hours until 3:00 AM after I realized it was time to get up. I glanced out my window, hoping he was sitting in his Nissan Pathfinder, but he was nowhere to be found.

I had other boyfriends in my life that brought me pain, joy and everything in between, but with him it was different. I felt him in my veins, blood, and body. With every move I made, he was in thought. With every word I spoke, his name was on my tongue. My emotions felt like they had been infiltrated and then quickly let go.

In the time it took for him to pack his things and leave, I went from knowing what I wanted to not even knowing who I was. In a split second, I reverted to the sheltered, scared and self-conscious eleven year old girl that needed her mother for every decision. I reached for the cordless phone with uncertainty.

"Hello?" I heard the sluggish voice say on the other line.

"Mama?" I said through my sniffles. I knew I'd gotten myself into this mess but I was hoping, by chance, mama could get me out of it.

She was, after all, the fixer of all my problems. When I was sick, she'd fix me a special potion and made me all better. When I was down and out, she sent the perfect card to lift my spirits. When I was low on funds, I could always count on mama to shoot a couple of dollars into my account without hesitation. When I needed help decorating my house, she was there with a smile on her face ready to help.

"Why should this be any different?" I thought, sitting down at the table and clearing my throat.

"Carmen, what's wrong?"

"It's late, Ma, and I'm sorry for calling," I sighed, pulling my knees to my chest and exhaling.

"I was awake anyway, baby. Is everything okay?" My mother lied. I heard her breathing heavily, a sign that she was probably sitting up in bed. My mom was the ultimate motherly figure with enough grace and class for ten women.

"I can call you back tomorrow."

"Talk to me!"

"He left me, Mama! He left!" I wailed, pounding my fist on the wooden kitchen table. I ran down the events from the night and cried over and over to my mother about everything I'd sacrificed, given and expected from the relationship with him. "How could he put me through something like this and make me feel this way?"

"Don't nobody make you feel inferior without your consent, baby," my mother said matter-of-factly. Her Mississippi roots came through the phone loud and clear.

"But, Mama, what do I do?"

"Listen to me, baby. He's gone now and good riddance to him. I've watched you as you've clutched to this imaginary relationship for years and I've stepped in and held your hand every time he left, every time he hurt you and every time the two of you had an argument! I will not do it anymore!"

"What do you mean?" I asked as my tears dried up.

"I mean *you* need to figure out what to do from here. It's only so much praying that I can do *for* you, baby. You've got to want better. Do you see how far off your path you've strayed?" she asked me.

I listened silently as the tears flowed down my cheeks and my head began to thump. It was tough to hear but I needed it.

"All your life you've loved the Lord and all your life you've served Him willingly and selflessly. But with *him* in the picture you've allowed *him* to become your God. You've allowed *him* total control and complete protection over you and that's why you're hurting. Can't no man protect you, do for you and love you the way that God can. you know that. Just think back to your life before him, baby," Mama said.

It sounded like she was crying with me. I knew it hurt her to hear me crying but she knew the strength in my tears.

"So what do I do, Mama?"

"Baby, it's all up to you to figure that out."

I held the phone tightly to my face. "I love you Mama," I said before hanging the phone up.

Emptiness overwhelmed me as I headed back into my bedroom. I plopped on the bed and threw my head into my hands.

Think back to your life before him, I recalled Mama's words. I got on my hands and knees and looked underneath my bed for the box of photographs, which I stored away, from my past.

Flipping the top off of the shoe box, I saw visions of myself that stared back at me. At first, though, I couldn't even recognize myself. I was cheery, happy and glowing. I could see the sparkle in my eye that I used to have and the energy that had somehow escaped me. Holding one picture up of me posing next to my mother in an oversized sweater and tights at Christmas time, I couldn't help but shake my head. I was an independent, college graduate who was going places and I was in love with God. Staring at myself in the mirror, in front of me, I knew exactly what Mama was talking about. I changed, but not for the better.

I wanted to be better and wanted better for my life, but I didn't know how. For almost three and a half years, I wanted someone that walked out on me and wasn't looking back. But I knew exactly what the first steps would be in order to get myself back.

I made my way to the shed in my backyard. Weeds rustled against my ankles as I struggled with the lock. I hadn't been out there since I first moved in here. Through my tears I could see what I was looking for: doors. The same doors I removed from my life around the same time I allowed him in. They were placed against a concrete wall with other moving boxes that I never got around to unpacking.

I heaved each door into the house one by one. I didn't care that it was late and my hands hurt. I didn't care that my head was thumping and my body was exhausted. I knew what I had to do. I went from door to door, room to room and screwed each door back on the hinges. Although I hated them, they were so much bigger than that.

As I struggled with my bedroom door, I closed my eyes and thought about who I became over the years. When I met him, I removed all the doors from my house as well as my heart and allowed myself to feel every emotion attached to him, raw but without God. But as he walked out of my life and my front door, I felt the sudden urge to protect my heart and reclaim what I lost.

I needed to guard my heart because as I started becoming someone I didn't recognize and doing things I couldn't understand. I neglected the very organ that kept me alive. I allowed my heart to handle all the excruciating labor while I sent it out into a battlefield without as much as a helmet on for protection. I realized I *did* know who I was and what I wanted and as much as it hurt, it wasn't him.

I followed his last order to me, hesitantly. *"Look at yourself,"* I heard his voice say in my head. Spinning around, I faced myself in the mirror. My slanted brown eyes were red and puffy from the hours of crying. My hair was a mess and my face looked swollen. I smoothed my shabby hair down and wiped clean the traces of mascara on my cheeks. Everything was hurting: my body, my heart, and most of all, my pride. But regardless of all the pain and disheveled appearance, I was still standing. I told myself that as soon as he was removed from my equation, air would cease to exist, taste would disappear and sound would have no meaning.

I was here, physically all alone, but I wasn't *alone.* God's presence was enveloped all around me. As I inhaled and proudly stood back admiring my finished bedroom door, a grin came over my face. It was nearing five in the morning and my eyes were growing heavy. I jiggled the door knob of my bedroom door and awkwardly opened it. Something sticking out from underneath my bed caught my attention. Reaching down, I picked the heavy book up and smiled. It was my Bible. The same Bible I tossed under the bed when I moved in. I swore I would read it daily, but never did so after all these years. I clutched the dark Bible with one hand and ran one finger over my name engraved in gold foil: Miss Carmen Sinclair.

Mama gave it to me when I was only six and it became my pride and joy. My heart sank as I thought how could I have forgotten about God in my quest for happiness? Hadn't I learned, been taught and prepared for the different disguises the devil might be in? As much as I thought I was ready for the enemy, no one could've convinced me that he would be six-foot-four and had lovely dreadlocks, a killer vocabulary, style, handsome features and a beautiful body.

I felt ashamed like I'd cheated on God with someone that didn't even give me half the love that I was used to receiving. I played myself, plain and simple, and now it was time for cleanup.

I noticed a gold plated bookmark inside the Bible. I pulled it out to get a better look. "Be still and know I am here," I said, reading the words printed on the bookmark.

I thought about how awesome God had been to me, even in the toughest of times. When my dad died, He was there to dry my tears. When I didn't get the job I knew I was perfect for me, He opened up a bigger and better door of opportunity. When I felt let down by him, God stepped through and showed that He was the only one in control. Somehow, I allowed the worldly memories to cloud the memories that God and I had together. I tolerated him being my weakness and allowed my faith in God to slowly vanish. Who was I?

The bookmark fell from my hands and into the Bible. I noticed how it had fallen perfectly underneath 2 Corinthians

12:9-10. My mouth dropped open as my finger followed each word of the passage I read aloud.

"But he said to me, My grace is sufficient for you, for my power is made perfect in weakness. Therefore I will boast all the more gladly of my weaknesses so that the power of Christ may rest upon me. That is why, for Christ's sake, I delight in weaknesses, in insults, in hardships, in persecutions, in difficulties. For when I am weak, then I am strong."

"Thank you, Lord!" I shouted. I clutched the Bible with both of my hands and felt the spirit pour over me with intensity as I cried tears of joy.

I wasn't able to see that God had brought me to and through my pain. He brought me to *him* and I had found my way back to the arms of the One who mattered the most. Hours ago, I couldn't imagine letting *him* go, now and stepping into the shoes of the woman I was. The reason God had allowed me to go through this phase was to bring me closer to his name. It was ultimately *my* plea. Not my Mama's,or my friends' pleas that brought me back safely. God revealed to me that within my weakness lied strength I didn't know was there.

I fell into bed and gazed at the ceiling. I could see the face of the man I knew as him. I jumped out of bed, raced to the open door, slammed it and quickly locked it. The next time it would be opened would be by the person with the key. Until then, I was content with the doors and protection that surrounded me. I closed my eyes and allowed God to sweep peace into my life.

WORD ON THE STREET
Jarold Imes

Seven young black men wearing black baseball caps that said Jesus Saves, long black T-Shirts, baggy but not sagging jeans and various brands of sneakers stepped out of the white, silver and maroon van. From a distance, they could have easily been mistaken for a reincarnation of the Wu-Tang Clan. By the way they attracted attention from the crowd, people at the nearby shopping center flocked to them expecting them to put on an impromptu rap concert in the middle of the street. After the last man stepped out and pulled the door shut, the driver of the van drove off cautiously trying to find a parking space near the barbershop at the top of the hill. The young men made their stop on this popular hill that was on the corner of Martin Luther King, Jr. Boulevard and New Walkertown Road of Winston-Salem.

Today was a Saturday, a day after payday and people were at this busy shopping center trying to catch fish dinners being sold by a local chapter of the Winston-Salem State University Alumni Association raising money for a Mr. Alumni contestant. Next to the fish vendor was a man who had faithfully sold hip hop inspired gear, and African American Art, and next to them, the sweet smelling soap from the make shift car shop greeted customers as they made their way up the hill to the shopping center. Well, some people never made it up the hill. In the intersection, members of the Nation of Islam were competing with a carrier to spread the news. Customers seemed to equally stop to support *The Winston Salem Journal* and the *Final Call*. It was there where Rahliem Victor, the leader of the Street Disciples Ministry Group sent half of the group.

Rahliem knew that his group was just a little over a mile from Winston-Salem State University and their home, Grace United Methodist Church. At the church, Rahliem was the lay leader and also vice committee chair for the outreach committee which Street Disciples Ministry Group spun out from. He made sure that each member had their maroon backpack filled with copies of *The Upper Room*, and a couple of books in their hands ready to pass out. Each of the young men who followed Rahliem out of the van, had come from various backgrounds and each had their own mission and method to spread the word of God in the hood.

Rahliem himself is a former convict who used to have problems with anger management. He learned how to calm down so that he could be the leader of the ministry God had placed on his heart. Since his time in the infamous Butler Juvenile Correctional Facility, he's learned to let the Holy Spirit guide his steps and keep his attitude in check. As he watched his boy, Donte "Longstocking" Speaks lead some of the young men who traveled with him to the busy intersection, he couldn't help but notice his nemesis, Minister Vincent X. Muhammad glaring at him. The two young men, who once were best friends, were known to get into public spats in the past. Rahliem looked away mainly to avoid the confrontation and argument over whose faith reigned supreme. Besides, Rahliem had to be a role model for the two new recruits he was left to train.

As Rahliem was passing out copies of *The Upper Room*, he noticed that Donte Speaks still was drawing a larger crowd of ladies who were more interested in him autographing their bootleg versions of his old videos from his former life. To these women as well as some of the men, Donte Speaks wasn't a man of God, but Donte "Longstocking," a man who knew how to, well, he doesn't talk about that aspect of his life anymore. Donte didn't make it any easier keeping by forgetting to wear the sun glasses that they had *just* stopped to the mall to pick up to avoid this incident. Rahliem knew that Donte would have it the hardest in spite of the fact that he was one of the first members of Street Disciples and the most experienced. But Donte knew that with this ministry, issues of his past as a local and famous adult video star would always come to play. Rahliem was just hoping that Donte wouldn't be asked to leave the corner as he had one time before. But being the true business man that Donte was, he had the ladies lining up along the sidewalk of New Walkertown Road just before the Wachovia branch.

Abednego Green wouldn't have an easier time. The rather short and somewhat stocky young man was a hustler at heart and great with words. Words that he used to convinced people to try his product became words that he would use to try to preach the Word of Christ. Abednego was good for reciting a quick Proverb or singing a verse of Psalms. Abednego was not afraid to stop passing out copies of the daily devotion to offer a quick word of prayer or to lead everyone in a soul stirring rendition of a Kirk Franklin or a Kiki Sheppard tune.

On the next intersection, Rahliem realized that Celtius remembered to bring his glasses. Unlike the other famous member of the Street Disciples, Celtius only wanted to be revealed by God. It had been over two years since Celtius chased after any man who told him he was beautiful. Any and everybody that had to do something with being a homosexual knew that Celtius was the man. Ironically, when Celtius got saved, the first thing he wanted to do was cut it off so he could be eunuch. He feared his member that much and called Rahliem and their Pastor Lauren Phelps every day for a quick five minute prayer session. Rahliem admitted that at first, Celtius got on his nerves about wanting to pray all the time; now, Rahliem and Pastor Phelps had concern when Celtius *didn't* call. Celtius led a class on celibacy and taught abstinence classes to the youth. Of course, his sexual orientation always came to question, but after a few minutes of talking to Celtius, there was no doubt where he stood in his relationship with God.

And at least Rahliem didn't have to keep Celtius and Mya from fighting anymore. Under no circumstances did Mya like homosexuals, even reformed ones like Celtius as he would say. Out of all the guys in the ministry, ironically, this church boy from Mississippi who led the choir was the one who almost didn't make the cut. Mya reminded Rahliem so much of his old self that it wasn't funny. Mya still sported that braids that made him look more like a girl than a boy. They are a few inches longer now that when Mya first joined. Mya had a very dangerous tongue that was lethal and no matter how many Bible verses you pointed out to the boy, he still had a hard time taming it. Rahliem hoped that this wasn't the thorn in his side that God wasn't removing, like that thorn he didn't remove from Paul. True, he couldn't spit game like Abednego could, but Mya could hold his own on the piano or with a guitar.

Standing next to Rahliem were Oscar and Calvin, two students from Winston-Salem State who were joining the campus ministry organized there. Oscar was a business man at heart and felt that the ministry would have been better served selling the devotions as opposed to giving them away for free. Oscar would have much rather stood on the corner with a bucket and a sign asking people to support the ministry. But Oscar also needed a lesson in humility and what better way to give it to him by having him serve other people, no charge of course. However, when you compare Oscar to Calvin, Oscar's issues were somewhat harmless. Calvin was a murderer. He killed a young man who terrorized him as a leader of a gang when he was twelve and some folks still say he's been a little off ever since. It wasn't that Calvin was off, he grew tired of folks asking him what it was like to kill somebody every fifteen minutes. Rahliem knew that when Calvin twisted his wedding band, he thought about it or was thinking about it. Part of the problem was that Calvin resented that fact that his older brother was *still* doing the time for his crime, even after he confessed it. Another issue was that he and his wife were having issues at home and dealing with how to raise their three year old boy who they just found out was diagnosed with cancer.

"I'm glad your little video star can keep his clothes on," Vincent stood next to him. Rahliem had been so busy passing out devotions and watching the members of his ministry that he didn't even noticed that Vincent had gotten next to him.

"I'm glad he is, too," Rahliem responded, "one should be fully clothed when doing the work of God."

"Whatever," Vincent responded to Rahliem's dismissal. "I don't see how you got all these crazy people and weirdoes supporting your ministry. Come on, Rahliem, you got a man for almost every deadly sin."

"Yet you are perfect?" Rahliem questioned. Before Vincent could make a comeback Rahliem replied, "I don't judge people on their past. That is not what Street Disciples is about. Street Disciples is about meeting people where they are, showing them the love that Christ has for them and bringing people together to make them useful contributors to the Body of Christ."

"Yeah, yeah, yeah, all that 'together as one' crap sounds nice, but are they really together as one?"

Rahliem pointed out each member of his ministry, "You see the books they are handing out this time?" He gave Vincent a chance to look and observe. "Regardless of whatever our personal issues may be, we come out here and give the people what they want, what they need in their lives. We come in peace. Just as you have, I presume?"

"I see you trying to save face in front of your friends," Vincent replied. I noticed him eyeing Oscar and Calvin and them returning grit in return. "You should have more love, joy, gentleness, goodness and all those other things you believe in. As-Salamu Alaykum."

"Wa Alaykum As-Salam."

Rahliem watched Vincent walk away and then stand at his post. Donte, Abednego, Celtius and Mya were making their way back across the street. They converged to the first table and interacted with the pastor of the Baptist church across the street. As Rahliem, Oscar and Calvin made their way to the table and getting their money ready for their own fish dinners, they enjoyed the comfort of fellowship in the name of the Christ that seemed to be taking place.

"Why did you greet him back?" Calvin asked.

"There is nothing wrong with responding back with the traditional Arab greeting. Yes, Muslims have adopted that as theirs, but the greeting has common and traditional meanings outside of Islam. Besides, he was wishing me peace and I wish him the same." Upon noticing an objection to his definition from Oscar, Rahliem continued. "I treat all people with the love of Christ. That is my outward sign of being a Christian. I can't profess to be a Child of The One Who Loves if I'm hating on everybody."

When the young men got to their table, they found that their meals were already paid for. A nice gesture on behalf of the candidate for Mr. Alumni, who happened to be a member of the church across the street.

"Elijah Phelps," he introduced himself to us. "Your pastor is my little sister. I'm proud to be supporting a ministry that is about uplifting people in the name of God and I'm even prouder to see my younger black brothers in the midst. Lauren used to say all the time that a child shall lead them."

"I still got a lot to learn," Calvin confessed, "back when I was younger, I never believed that people could get into the situations they found themselves in. Never understood how we could be so far away from Christ."

"It's not the situations that people find themselves in, it's in the way that they carry themselves in and ask God to work out their problems. And it doesn't hurt if they can follow directions either."

As they continued eating, a young lady came up and hugged Donte from behind. She must have spotted them from the street and observed where he was sitting. Donte turned around and in kind asked her how he knew her.

"Oh my gosh Donte, I'm like your number one fan!" she rambled, trying to sit in his lap. Donte was a little heated because he dropped some of the fish he was eating the ground. Realizing her mistake, she jumped up from her seat and apologized profusely for her actions. "I'm sorry, baby, I didn't see you eating! I hope you didn't swallow on a bone.

Donte quickly chewed on a piece of bread and swallowed the soft drink he was drinking. He wiped his face on the napkin and placed it gently beside his plate. "Not at all. What can I do for you?"

"I just want your autograph. I can't wait to tell my girls that I met Donte Longstocking in person!"

The name that made Donte millions has become the name that he has come to abhor. Nevertheless, Donte pulls out a copy of *The Upper Room* devotion, signs it and hands it to her. "I want to you to read today's devotion with your girls. If you agree with the message that God is bringing, come to our church on Sunday."

"Oooh, you gon' be there?!" The girl didn't hear a word of what he said about being at church or reading the message.

"Yes, I'll be there. And I hope to see you there too."

"Oh, I'm going to be there." She took the book and kissed him on the cheek. "Thank you so much and I can't wait to tell my girls to come and see you on Sunday."

The girl hastily ran across the street. Donte picked up the piece of fish off the ground, wrapped it up and placed it beside his nearly empty plate. He smiled and said, "It's too late for the five second rule."

"You handled that situation very well young man," Mr. Phelps commented, "I don't know too many people who would not have taken the opportunity to sit in the seat of judgment and talk about that woman."

"Well, I had to learn that with any mistake I have made that there is always a way to fix things. What I learned to do with my situation is to take each and every opportunity given to me when I meet a fan of the old me is to give them a chance to meet the new me. Sure, I get people that call me all kinds of names and say derogatory things about me, but for the few who take me up on my offer and come to church, have seen a change in their lives."

"Amen," Celtius added.

"It may not feel good, but it works out for my good."

"You always take an opportunity to share Christ with anyone young man, you never know whose listening."

As the young men finished eating, they cleaned up and got ready to go to our spots. They knew that everyone would stay on or near the intersection for a few more hours. Fortunately, their rep was strong enough to have a lot of repeat customers who came to find then so they could get their little leaflets or the large print versions of the books. Often times, some of the volunteers at the nearby Baptist church would allow them to operate from within their youth ministry room when the weather got too bad. The young men ran into community leaders, old friends and even a few celebrities and were often asked to speak everywhere. Rahliem, Donte and Mya were even involved in starting a second Street Disciples Ministry group in Greensboro to support the numerous colleges they had in the area.

Rahliem, Oscar and Calvin took their turn and joined Donte in operating from the intersection. Mya, Celtius and Abednego went on the hill. Upon seeing Rahliem on the Dr. Martin Luther King stretch, Vincent rushed over and switched places with the young man selling *Final Calls* on the street. Rahliem expected as much as they both were expected to be leaders of their respective groups. Rahliem disliked viewing their rivalry as part of some Christianity vs. Islam war but sometimes, he felt like he couldn't help but play into the feelings folks had about their run ins. A car came up bumping *And I* by Mary Mary featuring Kirk Franklin. Rahliem felt reassured that God was pleased with the work he was doing so he kept pressing on.

It was as surprise that Rahliem and Vincent avoided an altercation while working the same strip. Usually, the two just entered into a light disagreement about Jesus, Mohammed and whoever else there was to talk about. Today, Rahliem worked hard to get the people to receive a copy of *The Upper Room*. He was somewhat fortunate as the cover depicted African inspired characters and it did look fly. The usually uplifting set of devotionals focused on forgiveness and healing in this particular issue and that was what a lot of people needed.

When it was time to pack up and leave the street, Rahliem and the other young men headed straight to the van. They were surprised to see Mr. Phelps and their pastor having fun and laughing like they were little kids. They almost didn't see them coming.

"So how did the Street Disciples do today?" she asked. The pastor was excited and already anticipating good news. Each of the young men took off their back packs and looked at how many copies they had left.

"I only have twenty copies left," Donte proclaimed.

"And he signed half of them," Abednego added.

"I take it we'll have some young ladies joining the church this Sunday. That can be a good thing."

"I only have twenty, too," Rahliem said.

"I only have the large prints," Mya added. Truthfully, he forgot about the large prints in his bag. It was a blessing because the pastor knew she would need copies for Sunday Service.

"I got thirty five," Calvin added. His cell phone rang and he quickly picked up the phone to talk to his wife.

"I got thirty," Celtius added.

"I got thirty, too," Oscar finished counting. "People don't want free books like they used to."

"Well," the pastor interjected, "this wasn't a contest to see who could get rid of the most books. Our goal is to get the books into the peoples hands and to let them know that the devotions exist. I remember the first time we did this each of you had about seventy books left so we are improving with each issue."

"I got forty left," Abednego added. "I did spend some time praying with this older man at the church though."

"I knew you would be praying and singing with someone," she smiled. Abednego usually had the most books left. "This is the plan for next week when we go to Greensboro to meet with the young men interested in the ministry. We have enough books to show them how this works. Did we decide which street we were going to try and set up at?"

"Dudley and Market Street would be good," Donte answered. "That's right there where A&T is at, plus Bennett and Gilbert are down the street. The shopping center down south is black owned and a few of the shops have agreed to carry copies of the book."

"And we get to meet with the brothers on Friday night," Rahliem added. "We'll probably get some pizza or something and fellowship. May turn it into a Bible Study. I'm still working on my message for next Sunday too."

"You ready to give the Word, Rahliem?"

"I'll be ready with whatever the Spirit puts in front of me," Rahliem had gotten over being nervous about speaking the Word. Evidence of that was that Rahliem no longer stutters as much in his sermons.

"Well, don't feel like you have to rush the Spirit and come up with something right now. Let the message come to you."

Rahliem thought of the Pastor's words as he rode home. The van dropped everyone off at the church and he watched as each individual member got in their own cars and left the church.

Rahliem was finishing up washing the dishes from the vegetarian pizza and fruit salad he had for dinner when he heard a faint knock on the door. He assumed that either Celtius needed to hide out from one of his former boyfriends that was looking for him or that Calvin got put out of the house again. He was surprised at who he did see at the door.

"What's up, Vincent?"

"I'm good."

Gone was the black suit and bowtie. Vincent looked like Kanye West in his oversize sweater over a button up shirt and some baggy jeans. The oils he was wearing was strong and began to infiltrate his house before Vincent stepped foot in the door. Vincent took a seat on the couch and Rahliem sat across from him in the love seat. In spite being a minister of a Nation of Islam mosque in the city, Vincent actually came from a family of Baptist ministers. He converted to Islam when he was incarcerated while Rahliem focused more on building his relationship with Jesus.

"I swore when we got out of prison that I wasn't going back but Craig is going to send me there real quick."

Rahliem knew he was up for a long night when Vincent mentioned Craig. Craig Johnson was his sister's boyfriend/baby daddy. Craig and Vincent couldn't stand each other and have had numerous fights over everything from religion to how Craig abuses and mistreats his sister. Neither one of them are strangers to county jail either, doing bids at a time, usually over something one had done to the other.

"Let me get my keys and my shoes and I'll be ready in a minute."

Rahliem knew what Vincent's request was before he uttered the words out of his mouth. Truth is Vincent couldn't afford to be making too many more trips to jail or he risked losing his mosque. And as much as Rahliem wished Vincent would come back to his Christian roots and re-join a church, any church that was about the business of Christ, he wasn't going to let Craig be the reason Vincent went to jail either.

In no time, they were riding in his 2004 Nissan Sentra, making their way to Patterson Avenue. It was getting dark outside and various people walked up and down the street. Some were looking for a temporary home and others searching for night work. Vincent touched the beaded cross that was hanging from Rahliem's rear view mirror.

"When did you get this?"

"I've had it for about three months now. This lady down the street was making them and I figured I'd give her some support."

"They remind me of these rosary beads that Caryn used to have on her dresser." Caryn was Vincent's ex-fiancé before he got locked up. She stayed with him until he converted to Islam. Now she's dating a deacon of a church in High Point.

"Yeah, they kind of do, but they looked more African to me when I first got them."

Rahliem pulled up to the house that Craig and Vanessa were sharing. Craig was just leaving and he bumped into Vincent on the way out. Whether or not it was intentional or not, Vincent was two steps from making a decision that was going to put him back in county jail. Rahliem grabbed his arm and escorted him inside the house. A little five year old boy who just finished eating cake ran up to Vincent and gave him a big hug on his leg.

"Uncle Vinnie!" Vincent's nephew yelled in excitement. The little boy looked like a miniature version of Craig. Vincent put the boy down and he noticed his sister coming out of the kitchen.

"I see you brought reinforcement," Vanessa smiled at Rahliem. He looked around her house and admired her collection of black angels and church figurines that lined the mantle. Some of which must have been recently disfigured in Vanessa and Craig's latest fiasco.

"I needed to bring someone who I knew would keep me out of trouble and keep me grounded. Besides, I got to speak at the mosque next week and I can't put them through another incident leading me behind bars. I think they've been through enough."

"I do thank you and Rahliem for coming," Vanessa said, focusing on getting her shoes on and bringing some bags from a bedroom. "I need to get Junior and get out of here."

"You want to go back to Mom's?"

Rahliem was shocked that Vincent would make that suggestion. Vincent and his parents hadn't seen eye to eye since he announced he couldn't eat pork over the slab of ribs he had been offered for dinner.

"Yeah, but call first. You know they still think they are in their twenties and expect folks to warn them of emergencies this late at night."

"You didn't call them," Vincent responded with a little hint of frustration in his voice.

"I want to call granny and papa," Junior was making an already tense situation worse. Vanessa reluctantly left to make the call to her parents.

"I'm glad I didn't swing on that fool."

Rahliem cracked a smile. "You didn't look like you came to fight."

Vincent shook his head. "You always tried to doubt my skills in the ring, playa."

"But you remembered mine, though."

Both Vincent and Rahliem cracked a smile and grinned for a minute. The last time Vincent saw Rahliem get into a fight, they both went to jail for disturbing the peace among other things.

Vanessa rushed past them and got her bags. Vincent picked up Junior and they got up and got ready to go. Rahliem took Vanessa's bag and put them in the trunk of his car. Vincent rode with Junior in the back seat, leaving on the light in the back seat so he could read to him from the *Micky, Ticky Boo! Says Hello!* by Sabra Robinson. Listening to the two of them interact and discuss each of the characters, and their likes and dislikes, made the ride to Vincent and Vanessa's parents house easier. They noticed the light on in the middle of the street and their father waiting outside of the door. Rahliem popped the trunk and Vincent got his sister's bags out. Rahliem got cut off the engine and followed the family to their house. It had been almost ten years since he had been inside the Harper household, he almost felt like a little kid again waiting on Mrs. Harper to bring out freshly made cookies and a cup of water. The Harpers were a little tired, but they were happy that their daughter and grandson were safe from harm for the night.

After making sure that Vanessa and Junior were situated, Vincent cut the trip short and he and Rahliem went back to Rahliem's place.

"Good looking out for taking me to my sister's house."

"Anytime, man, anytime. I'm going to have to go back to get Mrs. Harper to bake me a batch of cookies."

"Yeah, Mom hasn't baked any cookies in a long time."

The rest of the ride to Rahliem's house was silent. It was hard to believe that these two friends could be on two different paths spiritually. Rahliem was just happy that he got to spend another day spreading the Word of God and he hoped that God was pleased with his actions as he dealt with the new members of Street Disciples and Vincent. Before Vincent pulled out of the driveway, he said a quick prayer hoping that the young man made it home safely and he even prayed that Craig was safe and out of trouble wherever he was at. In a few hours, it would be Sunday and he knew he had to get some rest. He opened up *The Upper Room* and began to re-read the day's scripture from Matthew 7:3-4:

"Why do you look at the speck of sawdust in your brother's eye and pay no attention to the plank in your own eye? How can you say to your brother, "Let me take the speck out of your eye," when all the time there is a plank in your own eye?"

He thought of the day's lessons and quickly came up with a devotion that he may use for his sermon next week.

One Woman's Journey
Linda R. Herman

Once upon a time. I figure, if I started with that beginning, I could end with happily-ever after. Once upon a time, I had Craig and hopes of a family, but now Erica, his twenty year old devoted white secretary, has my man and she's having his child. So, where did that leave me? Yep, that left me sitting here, at my small dining room table in the apartment I shared with my girlfriend Zora with a glass of wine in one hand and a bottle of sleeping pills in the other.

Craig promised to always be there for me. He was my rock and my world. When I lost my parents in a tragic car accident, Craig was there. He promised that I would never be alone. Knowing how much I adored them, he promised that he loved me as much as they did. I believed him, needed him, and revolved my world around him.

Recurring nightmares invaded my psyche and waves of agony flooded my heart whenever I thought about my parents' death. Craig and I had invited them to join us for dinner at Red Lobster in Albany. We were celebrating Craig's first big case. We didn't all travel together because Craig wanted to drive his brand new Corvette instead of my Acura. My parents drove their Town Car with no complaints. We were enjoying a lovely evening. Both Craig and my father had a few drinks too many, but my father insisted on driving even though my mother tried to persuade him not to.

"Nate, let me drive. You've had too much to drink," my mother insisted.

"Catherine, I drive better when I'm feeling good," my father joked.

Craig gave me his car keys without putting up a fuss. The last thing he wanted to do was wreck his brand new baby.

We were almost back in Crisp County when the accident occurred. My father appeared to be driving fine. My mother and I were talking with each other on our cell phones when I heard her yell, "Nate, look out!" I looked in the rearview mirror in time to see my parents' Lincoln turned sideways across the two lane roadway. An eighteen-wheeler hit them fast and hard. Before I could turn around, there was a loud explosion as their car burst into flames. I desperately wanted to free them from the burning car, but Craig said that it was too late. They were already dead.

I cried my heart out the entire time at the closed casket funeral while Craig held me in his arms. My girls, Monica and Zora were there for me as well, but no one could comfort me. I lost a big part of my identity. The reason for my very existence was now dead and gone, only to remain with me in spirit. My foundation had been taken away from me. It was all because my father swerved to miss a damn deer!

I became absorbed in Craig's life. Every aspect of me revolved around him. He was my center and my core. Without Craig, I was just an empty, lifeless shell. He told me how much he loved me and would never leave me.

"Liar!" I screamed, opening the bottle and pouring all the pills out on the table. "He's a bold face liar!"

Why shouldn't I kill myself? What did I have to live for? Craig didn't give a damn about me. I was the one who was by his side through thick and thin. It was my earnings that kept our utilities on and food on the table. Back in the day, we were eating peanut butter without jelly on saltine crackers. I worked full time and contributed to his education. He worked part time as a paralegal and didn't contribute to any bills or household expenses. But as soon as Craig got a taste of filet mignon, he shattered my heart. Tears fell from my eyes as I tthought about the painful day that I lost the love of my life and my will to live.

It was our third wedding anniversary. I went to his office to surprise him with a basket of soul food. I had spent all morning cooking all of his favorites: fried chicken, collard greens, baked macaroni and cheese, green beans, potato salad, ham, cornbread, and for dessert, banana pudding. I was looking forward to a night of passionate lovemaking with my sexy husband. He was too busy with work that we had not been intimate in months.

I stepped off the elevator with a proud smile on my face because I was Craig's wife. I carried the basket filled with our lunch and a pitcher of sweet iced tea with sliced lemons. Since it was a warm April day, I hoped we would have lunch outside at Watermelon Park to celebrate our anniversary.

I noticed that Erica wasn't at her desk. Assuming she went to lunch, I sat the basket down at her desk and walked into my husband's office still carrying the pitcher. I expected him to be hard at work on a conference call with legal papers covering his desk. Not wanting to disturb him, I didn't knock and quietly entered his office. Instead of finding Craig hard at work, I found Erica down on her knees in front of his desk hard at work. Craig sat there moaning with his eyes closed, obviously enjoying his secretary's oral skills. My chest hurt with every breath I took. My knees buckled and I shook uncontrollably. The pitcher of tea fell from my grasp and shattered. Tears spilled from my eyes as the icy liquid quickly covered the floor. It was then that he opened his eyes and saw me standing there.

"Amber! My God, what are you doing here?" Craig asked, standing up, zipping up his pants and pulling away from Erica. She wiped her filthy mouth with the back of her hand and tried to walk out of the office past me. She actually thought she could just walk away. Wrong!

I blocked the door and locked the three of us in. "You're not going anywhere," I told her. She begged for me to let her pass, but I wouldn't allow it. I was so overcome with anger, rage, and pain, I didn't even know if I punched or slapped her as I tried to recall what happened after she went down. Who did she think she was trying to seduce my husband? It was our anniversary! I should have never trusted her sweet words and phony smile. Women these days were looking for men who were already established. They didn't want to support a man who was on the rise, the way I was supportive of Craig. Earning my rightful place as his wife, I would beat her to death before I let her walk away with my man.

My husband frantically rushed around his desk and grabbed me off her. He instructed her to call security on *me*. I was only protecting what was mine in an attempt to save our marriage. The irony of it all was that he was threatening to press charges against me for assaulting his lover!

"I'm not in love with you, Amber! I've tried to show you that but you act like you're too stupid to get it!" he yelled just as security rushed in. "Do you get it now?" In front of Erica and the security guards, Craig dehumanized me. He stripped me of every ounce of pride that I had. I felt so humiliated but still I couldn't let go.

Still, I did something I promised myself I would never do. I begged. On bended knee, I foolishly pleaded with him. I didn't care that I was in a puddle of tea, broken glass and squishy lemons ruining my brand new outfit. I just wanted Craig's love.

"Please don't leave me! You promised me! You promised that you would always be

there for me! I'll kill myself if you leave me!" I threatened. I then promised to do anything he asked. I even told him I was okay with his affair because I loved him and I just wanted him with me. I wanted him even if it meant sharing him with her.

"Amber, I can't bring your parents back," he said without emotion, knowingly opening a wound that wasn't completely healed. "I know how much you loved them but life goes on.

I'm not going to stay in a relationship with you just because you can't get over their deaths," he said dismissively with a shrug of his shoulders. "I've got my own life to live and I'm tired of babysitting you."

Security picked me up off the floor but my pride was left down there in the midst of the floor's mess and salty tears. They carried me out of his office kicking, screaming, and crying. All I wanted was for him to run to me and say he was sorry and that he loved me. I was ready to forgive and forget. It didn't happen. Instead he yelled, "You're pathetic! Go get counseling or something!"

Craig kicked me out of *our* home, because like a fool, I signed a prenuptial agreement. I wanted to convince him that my love was pure. I didn't care about the money. It was the man that meant more to me than my own life. So, despite the years that I worked and supported us, I walked away with far less than I entered into the marriage with. I walked away with the clothes on my back. My dignity and self respect were nowhere to be found.

I doubt the ink was even dry on our divorce papers before he married Erica. And now, less than a year later, she was about to give birth to his child. I wanted to be the mother of his children, but he had told me to wait. I waited because he kept telling me to wait since he wasn't ready for children. For me, he wasn't ready; for her, the time was right.

"What did she have that I didn't?" I asked myself, finishing my fourth glass of wine. "She's younger but I'm not old. She's twenty or twenty-one now. I'm only thirty-one. That's not old.

She's white but she's not as pretty as I am. Didn't anyone ever tell him that black is beautiful?" I tried to laugh at my own joke but instead more tears fall from my already puffy eyes.

I stared at the pile of pills. I tried so hard to find a reason why I shouldn't take them. Tired of all the sadness and emptiness, I refilled my glass of wine and scooped up the pills. I didn't want to think about Craig and Erica anymore or have any nightmares about my parents dying. I wanted to end my pain and misery.

"Amber! Amber, what are you doing?" I wasn't expecting Zora home so early. I

thought I could take my pills and slip away quietly. But here she was snatching pills out of my mouth and hands.

"I just wanna be with my parents, Zora! I can't take being here in so much pain!"

Zora held me close to her and listened to me cry about my shell of a life. She heard all of this before, but she let me talk without interruption. I didn't know how long I cried, but when I woke up the next morning in my bed, she was still cradling me in her arms.

"I'm sorry about last night," I said, trying to smooth my unkempt hair down with my fingertips. I knew I must look a mess. I smelled terrible and my mouth felt icky.

"You don't have to apologize to me, Amber. I'm your friend and I'll always be here for you," Zora assured me, offering me a hairbrush.

"No, you won't. You're going to move out in a few weeks and leave me alone, too." Zora was engaged to her fiancé, Marc. I was happy for her that she had found true love, but I also resented her because she would be leaving me alone. I wasn't ready to be alone.

"It doesn't matter where I live. I'll always be here for you." she said, ignoring my attitude which was typical of her. "Why don't you get dressed and come to church with me? My brother is doing his trial sermon today."

"I fell out with God when he took my parents away from me. Craig was my God. Then he left me as well. I have no place in church."

"Don't you even go there!" she warned. Zora didn't play around about God. Her father was a preacher and her late mother was a Sunday school teacher. "The problem in your marriage was what you just said. You allowed Craig to be your God. There's only one God, Amber, and He tells us not to put no man before Him. You put Craig before Him and everyone else. You worshipped the ground that man walked on and even to this day, you haven't let him go." She took me firmly by both arms. "Let him go! I could suggest that you get counseling, but the truth is you don't need it. You need to amend your relationship with God, Amber. You have got to stop blaming Him for your parents' death. I lost my mother, but I don't blame God, because I know it was just her time to go. I thank Him for freeing her of the pain that the cancer caused her. I know she is up in Heaven looking down on me. Don't you know your parents are up there looking down on you?"

I could only shrug my shoulders because I was sobbing and crying.

"Why do you think I got here before you swallowed those pills?"

I couldn't answer her and shruggled my shoulders again.

"God is not done with you and if I have anything to say about it, you're not done with Him either. So get yourself in the shower because you're going to church if I have to drag you there kicking and screaming!"

I didn't argue with Zora on those rare occasions when she became angry. We arrived at church an hour later. It was the first time I've been in a church since my parents' funeral. As a child, I spent every Sunday in church sitting beside my mother. As Craig's wife, I spent every Sunday catering to him.

I listened to the choir sing familiar songs. I remembered the words to most of the selections. I was starting to feel pretty good about being here. I wouldn't even mind being up in the choir stand with Zora.

Pastor Larry Anderson, Sr, Zora's father, stood up and addressed the congregation. At fifty-one, he was still a very attractive man. One wouldn't believe he was the father of thirty-one year old Zora, and thirty-three year old Leroy, Jr.

"Today, I am happy to have my son, Leroy, Jr. here with me," he said, looking back at his son. "Most of you know him as LJ. He's been living out of state for awhile, but God has brought him back home to Cordele. Today he's here to preach his very first sermon." Everyone applauded as LJ stood beside his father. The two men could have been mistaken for twins. "It makes a father proud to have his only son follow in his footsteps. It truly is a blessing from the Lord and I thank Him!" Again, we all applauded as the older Anderson embraced his son.

LJ was looking educated and sophisticated in his double breast suit and eyeglasses. He was always smart, but I didn't remember him being so handsome. In school, he was what we kids referred to as a nerd. He wore thick glasses that made his eyes look twice as big as they really were. He also wore braces for awhile and then he wore a retainer.

He wasn't really ugly, but when he invited me to the prom in his Senior year, I couldn't help but to laugh in his face. He ended up taking his sister, Zora. Things did certainly changed though. His eyeglasses were very stylish and his teeth were not only straight, they were pearly white. He looked great.

"It truly is a blessing to be back in my Father's house," he said. "Good evening to all of you."

The congregation returned his response.

"I'd like to ask that you all bear with me today because as my father said, this is my trial sermon. So, if I don't move you today, my father won't let me preach for you again."

We all laughed at his cute little joke. The more he talked, the more I found myself attracted to him. It was more than his looks. His words were touching me. He was reading from Exodus and the words were a reflection of my earlier conversation with Zora.

"And God spake all these words, saying, I am the Lord thy God, which have brought thee out of the land of Egypt, out of the house of bondage. Thout shalt have no other gods before

me. Thou shalt not make unto thee any graven image, or any likeness of any thing that is in heaven above, or that is in the earth beneath, or that is in the water under the earth. Thou shalt not bow down thyself to them, nor serve them: for I the Lord thy God am a jealous God, visiting the iniquity of the fathers upon the children unto the third and fourth generation of them that hate me; And showing mercy unto thousands of them that love me, and keep my commandments. Thou shalt not take the name of the Lord thy God in vain; for the Lord will not hold him guiltless that taketh his name in vain." He closed his Bible and removed his glasses. "I have read to you Exodus, the twentieth chapter, verses one through seven. Our God is a jealous God and we are told to put no other God before thee." He paused, looking out at the congregation. "Some of us have not taken heed to the Word."

He was talking to me. I was guilty of putting Craig, whom I deemed my own god, first in my life. I needed to hear the words that he was speaking. He preached on and his words sunk deeply into my spirit and touched my soul. By the time he concluded his sermon, I was in tears. I didn't feel empty or alone. I felt God in my spirit and I was crying tears of joy because the Holy Spirit was dwelling within me again. First, there was pain, then there was numbness, but now there was joy.

The choir sang *Thank you Lord* as the congregation rose to their feet.

"If there be anyone amongst us today, who feel they're in need of prayer, come to the altar," LJ said, wiping sweat from his forehead with his handkerchief. "It doesn't matter what kind of situation you're in, God can answer your prayers. All you have to do is come to Him."

Several people filed to the front of the church and knelt at the altar. I pushed forward to join them. It was time to let Craig go because I couldn't keep holding onto him. It was time that I fully acknowledge my Heavenly Father and obey His word. I fell to my knees and asked for God's forgiveness. I didn't feel humiliated the way I did when I was begging Craig. I felt elated and free. I felt my pride restored when I rose from the floor.

"It's so good to see you again," LJ said after service.

"It has been a long time," I replied, offering him my hand to shake. He pulled me in for a brotherly hug. I tried not to feel all tingly, but I couldn't help it. He smelled so good. I hadn't been held this close by a man since Craig.

"I'm proud of you. I hope you'll come back," he whispered in my ear.

I assured him that I would do so. Zora and Marc came over and insisted that I join them for dinner at their father's home. I tried to get out of it, but I couldn't tell a lie in the church.

"So, what's been going on with the beautiful girl who laughed in my face when I asked her to the prom?" LJ asked me at dinner. I nearly choked and his family all laughed at my embarrassment.

"I'm sorry about that, LJ. I should have apologized years ago. That was very rude and inconsiderate of me." I couldn't believe he brought that up.

"I didn't mean to embarrass you, Amber. It's in the past. I don't hold it against you." He took a sip from his lemonade. "You know, I've been in love with you since the first day that you came over to play with Zora. I told my father that I loved you and I asked him what I should do about it."

"I remember that day," Pastor Anderson said.

"Yep, and he gave me the best advice. He told me to pray about it and believe in my prayer. So, that's what I did. I prayed for you, Amber and I never gave up."

I was so nervous that I didn't know what to do. I felt butterflies in my stomach. I looked to Zora for help, but she and Marc appeared as shocked as me. I opened my mouth to speak, but I didn't know what to say. I never thought of LJ in that way. Now that he was a pastor, I wasn't sure if I should be thinking of him in that way. I was attracted to him, but I didn't know if it was okay for me to feel that way. All eyes were on me. I didn't even know if I was ready for a relationship. And if so, was I worthy of being with a man of God?

"I'm not asking you to marry me. Well, at least not today," LJ told me with the slightest parting of his lips which melted my insides. "I don't know everything that has happened with you, but I can tell that you've been hurt. I know you need time to get over that. All I'm asking is that you let me be there for you. I just want to be a shoulder to cry on and a friend to reassure you that with God, this too shall pass."

The sincerity of his words caused my eyes to water. He wanted to be my friend. As much as I loved and worshiped Craig, he never treated me like a friend. He just enjoyed all the things that I was willing to do to please him.

"Only when you're ready, I want to be your husband. I want to shower you with my love and let you know every single day that you are a beautiful and wonderful woman. I want you at my side to grow with me. There's so much we can teach each other as we learn more and more about God. I want you to take this Christian walk with me, Amber. Will you?" LJ extended his hand to me.

Was I worthy? I turned away from him and lowered my head. "I don't know what I have to offer you, LJ. I've just found my way back to God. I'm ashamed to say that when I lost my parents, I was angry at Him. Then I allowed a man to be my god. I really don't know what if anything I can teach a man like you. I'm not even sure if I deserve someone like you."

"Just say yes, Amber. Just say that you'll take this Christian walk with me. The rest is in God's hands. He will forgive you, but you have to also forgive yourself. And know that you do deserve to be loved."

I heard his words. The words spoken by a man who proclaimed not only his love, but also his respect for me as a person. I didn't know if I'm ready, but I had to put my faith in God. Something in my spirit told me that God himself sent this man to me even before he became the man who sits before me.

So, in that very moment, I let go and I let God. I let go of all the humiliation and the pain that had consumed me. I let God open my heart to a wonderful man who knew my worth as a woman. I said yes. I accepted his hand and I joined LJ in his Christian walk. He gave me the time I needed to get my relationship with God back on track. He was there for me every step of the way. And when I was ready, he became my husband.

He kept his promise. He showered me with his love and every single day he told me that I was a beautiful and wonderful woman. I learned to love myself. I learned, through my husband and the Almighty that if I loved myself, I didn't have to seek it in another man's eyes.

Together we've grown so much in our faith. We taught our three kids all about God. My favorite contribution was my very own personal journey. *Thou shalt have no other gods before me.* Exodus 20:3. And now, I could honestly say, my life was happily ever after because with God, I could weather any storm.

I'M STILL HERE
Kim Robinson

After everything I have been through, it took me getting to the age of forty-seven to realize that God had a plan for me all along. I speak at churches now letting others know that they can change their lives as I have done. Standing up at the front of a room with all those faces looking up at me with both hope and desperation in their eyes, further encourages me to keep pushing forward. I know that what I have to say will help people know that they are still here because of God, and as long as they are, God has a purpose for them; they just need to find it and be obedient.

People ask me, "How I can speak so candidly about my past?" I tell them that speaking to others is the only thing that gives me and my past purpose.

I was brutally raped by a preacher at the age of five. Traumatized, confused and scared, the preacher took advantage of it all. His shameful programming was, "If you tell anyone, everybody you know and love will die and go to hell." From that day, I took everyone's illness as something that I had caused. I felt the shame and guilt, and though I did not tell anyone, I wanted to tell my father, but those words just kept running through my mind. Six months later, I was told that he was going to die, though he is still alive today, I felt like it was my fault that he spent so much time in the hospital.

For thirty years, I suppressed the memory of the rape somewhere behind a door in my mind.

When I was old enough to discover drugs, they helped me to keep that door closed. Drugs helped me to ease the pain that was growing and festering like cancer in my soul. When I was high, I could feel no pain. No memories would consume me whole. No shame, no guilt, no betrayal.

I felt like God did not like me and I did not like Him. I refused to go inside of a church and I would not read the Bible or listen when people spoke of religion. God was no friend of mine. If God was the God everyone said He was, then why would he let a precious five year old little girl go through so much turmoil?

All my life people told me that I was going to do things to help bring others to God. Every time I heard it, I thought those who said it were out of their minds. Because, by this time, I was in the life of prostitution and drug dealing which meant I wasn't saving anybody, not even myself.

I spent my whole life breaking the law in one way or another, from the youth program that I hustled for to scamming insurance companies, selling drugs and hot clothes. My life was a serious roller coaster ride between the penitentiary, dodging bullets, and being stabbed. Having to look over my shoulder every day was a way of life.

One of the worst times in my life was when I had to put my three year old son on a bus to go back to California from Vegas.

The guy that I was seeing at the time had brought a girl into my apartment while I was away working the fight. I had a lot of drugs there and my name was on the lease and when she got busted she set him up. There was a warrant out for my arrest. I had a choice; either go to jail for thirty five years or run for seven.

My baby, that I had spent just about every day with, would not see my face for seven years, and hearing my voice was just not enough.

Working my way across the country on my back was not much fun either. Not to mention, leaving my family and the only state I had lived in for twenty six years. I was forced to work the street just to keep us in hotels; until I could make enough contacts with the escort services to keep us afloat. Half the time, I could not work because I was too battered and bruised from the beatings he gave me.

So many people in my life would smile in my face, but I couldn't turn my back to them. People were in my life to hurt me. At the time, I couldn't see anything, except for the hustle. Again, I needed to survive, and I needed to block out anything hurtful in my mind. But when I truly think about it, I often wonder if my self-hatred came as a result of my abuse? Is that why I continuously abused myself by living this life? And is it the same abuse that I allowed others to do to me? Like my grandmother said, "What goes around comes around and you reap what you sow." I was planting some awful seeds, and so were the so-called friends around me.

ھ ھ ھ ھ ھ

He had been on the run for years and when he decided to go back to Texas his brother dimed him out and the feds got him. Life got a bit better when I landed in Oahu, running twenty one girls and a tour agency. That turned to crap too when the little girl that I was taking care of while her mom was in jail wound up raped, mutilated and murdered right alongside of her ice head mother.

Adding insult to injury, I was kidnapped and held for ransom. Two girls that worked for me were thrown from a thirtieth floor balcony and the police invited me to leave and I went back to Texas. It was a continuous downward spiral of events, Until...

I met a wonderful man who gave me a new view on life. I was away from all the hustling and drama. I had even stopped getting high. Being with him made me happy. It was a wonderful fairy tale romance.

Unfortunately, the life caught up with me, I had a client that I had seen for years in California and he had tracked me down and wanted to resume our relationship. I was four months pregnant when he approached me. I explained that I was not tricking anymore, but he had all the information on my man who was an executive and I was not going to ruin his life after he had saved mine.

Being forced to succumb to the extortion was more than I had ever had to deal with in twelve years of working. I started getting high just to deal with the situation. An all too familiar solution to my problems was getting high, going back into a life of hiding from fears and bad memories.

I tried to reason my way out. I tried to pay my way out, but he still kept demanding to see me. After I gave birth to my son, he left me alone for awhile, then he told me to bring my child. I was not going to do that. That was a turning point for me. A crossroads. When I was forced to get my son involved, it made something click in my mind.

Well I contacted some people who handled the situation, and though I was out of it, I kept seeing this man's spirit. It would not stop haunting me. I could not take it anymore and I figured that if I took myself out of the equation, none of the people I loved would be hurt because of my past. I caused too much pain to all those who loved me.

I slit my wrist. The pain became way too much to bear. Agony settled deep down in my spirit, and it took over my life. I wanted to end it all; a life full of pain and trauma. Needing to put a cease order on all of the trouble, chaos, the bad memories, suicide was a viable option. One that I thought would end my agony, and also one that would alleviate any more hurt I caused my family.

By the grace of God, my man found me. Yes, I did acknowledge God. I ended up in rehab where I found out that God had not sent that preacher to rape me. That man had nothing to do with God. After spending three months in rehab, I soon realized many things. The most crucial was that God had been in my life all along. When I was released from rehab, the therapist told me that I had to find a church home.

I finally got up enough nerve to go to church. Extreme discomfort is what I felt upon entering the church. Going through those church doors, I could see all eyes on me. People looked at me sideways.

God put people in my life at the church to help me. There was one woman in particular that I felt so comfortable talking to. And, after a few months of going to church and speaking with this woman, I was comfortable. It was my home away from home. I often wondered what took me so long to get to this beautiful place. And this woman, after hearing my story she told me, "You are still here and you are still standing, God has a purpose for you."

For the first time I believed it. I believed God had a true purpose for me. Writing down my feelings everyday was cathartic. It was a healing for me. I got involved with the women's ministry and started receiving phone calls from people asking me to talk to women who were still out turning tricks or doing drugs. My hard life prepared me to go out on a mission to help save women whose shoes I was once in. My soul felt an awakening after speaking to these lost souls. Helping these women was the greatest gift I could give, and I felt like the words that came out of my mouth were not from me but from God.

When I stand up in front of a church, I don't practice any speech, I just open my mouth and let what God wants me to share come out. I thought someone was playing a joke when I was asked to speak at the abused women's ministry at the Potters House. When I stood there talking, I felt like my life had come full circle and every terrible thing that had happened to me in my life had brought me to that moment, doing the thing that God put me here to do.

Helping someone escape pain or abuse, let's me know that "I am still here and I am still standing."

God is an awesome God, and if you continue to trust and believe, there are infinite possibilities.

THE TRIUMPH OF MY SOUL
Elissa Gabrielle

P ush! Mary, push a little harder. You're almost there!"
In the heat of the night on a hot, humid and muggy
August evening, Mary Thomas, rested on her elbows
as sweat and fear drained from her brow as she gave birth to
her fourth child. The white walls of the delivery room became
dizzying after countless hours of intense, brutal labor pains. The
doctors in the medical center provided her only comfort on that
night—a terrifying, yet joyous night in August of 1973.

Mary lived a hard life, not due to her own self-infliction,
but rather at the peril that came from life's circumstances. She
wondered, at that moment, as she laid in agony, why she decided
to bring another life into the world, considering the state of the
world in 1973.

It was just a few years earlier that Mary witnessed life-altering
realities, smack dab in her face, in her own backyard. For Blacks
in 1967, Newark was a place of deplorable conditions. The city
had a multitude of problems that range from social, psychological,
political and of course, economical. The politicians weren't
doing much to help this community in need. So the community
of Newark, New Jersey who had the largest Black population

in the Northeast at that time were fed up. Their feelings of being disrespected by whites and the police had come to a boil. In July 1967, Newark, New Jersey was in the midst of the worst race rebellion since the riots in Watts that took place a couple of years earlier.

In the midst of excruciating, physical pain, Mary pushed harder, as she looked down to see one white male doctor, dressed in blue scrubs, and thick-rimmed glasses, hoping to find comfort in his words.

"Come on, Mary, you can do it! I can see the head."

"Oh God, I'm trying! Ooooooh!" Mary screamed as the tears poured profusely from her eyes.

A black nurse patted Mary's forehead with a cold, damp, washcloth, and told her to breathe. "Inhale through your nose, Mary, and exhale through your mouth."

Mary looked deep into the nurse's eyes, and yelled, "I can't! It hurts!"

"You can do it, Mary!" the nurse whispered softly, trying to calm her down.

"Aaaaaah!" Mary screamed a heart-wrenching yell.

Terror filled the room moments after Mary's groan. All's to be heard was the doctor's voice that yelled to the nurse, "The baby is in distress!" He rushed from the place he was sitting, in preparation of delivery of another human life, instead he flew to grab an instrument to aid him in getting the child into the world alive. The responsibility that laid on his shoulders was intense and he knew he not only held Mary's life in his hands, he also had the burden of delivering the child, a healthy child.

Blood poured continuously from Mary's womb onto the operating table. The nurse, in a heated panic, yelled, "Oh God!" as she rushed over to assist the doctor.

"What's wrong with my baby?" Mary screamed and questioned as she tried to get up off of the table. The nurse then moved in closer to Mary, gently restrained her and made her relax.

"The baby is in distress, but everything will be okay," she expelled, while caressing Mary's hand.

Heavy sobs left Mary's now lifeless body, as she went into shock.

"Doctor! We're losing her," the nurse spewed, tears flowing down her cheeks.

With a pair of forceps, the doctor carefully pried the baby from Mary's limp body. A team of physicians were by the baby's side, as they planted her on the table, clearing her airways. The sound only God could create left the baby girl's mouth as she yelled to the world, informing everyone of her safe arrival.

"You have a girl. A healthy, baby girl," the doctor smiled as he handed Mary her daughter.

"She didn't make it, doctor," the nurse sorrowfully revealed, as she took the baby from the doctor, and gently placed her onto her mother's breast.

෫ ෫ ෫ ෫ ෫

I often wondered why God would allow my mother to deliver me, yet succumb in the process. Women take for granted the miracle of childbirth. I was told, many times over, that I should have died right on that table with my Mom. Retractors said she shouldn't have brought another child into the world, especially living on a dollar and a dream. Favoring my Mother, from the top of her head to the tips of her toes, there's no denying that I'm her daughter. Long, wavy, black hair, full lips and a round, caramel-kissed face, makes me a spitting image of Mom.

The day I came home from the hospital was the same day I was handed over to the State's social workers. Failure to provide a stable environment, and no real family to sustain her, my Mother raised three girls, excluding me, on the salary of a waitress. Her love for spoken word and the gift of song, made her uniquely wonderful, enticing to others, but it failed to pay the bills.

My Dad was one of my Mother's fans, and pursued her to no end. He beat her so severely the night of my birth, on that hot and dizzying August night.

Growing up in one foster home after another exposed me to drugs and death, and despair, to molestation and to hell and back. And through the fire, my Mother's voice would keep me calm. Even in my tender years, I felt her presence. It kept me sane. My mother's love for poetry was innately passed from her bloodstream to mine and throughout my life, I would write and it was cathartic.

After nine years of life and four foster homes, I ended up with Mrs. Mosley, a drug-addicted mother, whose only reason for keeping me was to get a guaranteed five hundred dollars a month. So, eventually, five hundred dollars a month was all I was worth.

I remember one morning in the fall of 1983. I just turned ten years old and still resided with Mrs. Mosley; an older black woman with dark circles that rested under her eyes. Her jheri-curled auburn hair piled loosely across her head, with ringlets that danced around her brows. Large, buck, yellow teeth were hidden behind a set of blackened lips, the kind of lips that discolored from smoking cigarettes for decades. She wore the same pink, flowery housedress all day, every day, even when she had to pick me up from school when I would misbehave. One day in particular stays with me.

"Hey, girl! Get your tail in here! Got me coming to school, wasting my time, and interrupting my soaps. Don't you know One Life To Live is on!" Mrs. Mosley snatched me up by my long ponytail, one that I so carefully brushed that morning myself. See, she never did my hair, or bathe me, or wash my clothes; I always took care of myself, I was left no choice.

"Yes, M'am?"

"Don't you "Yes M'am" me little girl!"

Dragging me across the living room floor, she took me from one room through the next until I finally ended up at the back door, which led to a flight of stairs, which led to the basement. The wood that entered my back from Mrs. Mosley's floor, splintered into my flesh and Lord knows I wanted to scream, but I didn't. I would've taken a worse beating had I spewed a sound.

"You stay your behind down there," Mrs. Mosley fussed as she threw me down the stairs. Landing at the foot of the stairs, I glanced up to see Mrs. Mosley slam the oak door, and all faded to black. I sat in that corner and cried for what seemed like a lifetime, until I was interrupted by Lora gasping for air.

"Alicia?" she yelped between breaths.

"Lori? Is that you?" I asked as I felt her presence near.

"Where are you, Lori?"

"I'm in the basement, Alicia."

In the darkness, I felt my way down the stairs and into the basement of that cold, clammy, rotting room I'd grown so familiar with. I wondered for some time where Lori, another foster child in Mrs. Mosley's care, had gone. Here she was all along.

Reaching her, I was happy to see her again, but terrified that I too was now in the same situation as Lori.

"Are you okay, Lori?" I asked, while rubbing her forehead and moving the hair from her face.

"I'm so hungry, Alicia," she cried between gasps. I imagined, through the darkness, the terror in Lori's dark brown eyes. I saw her streaming tears flow down her chocolate covered cheeks, in my mind's eye. Lori's severe asthma would kick in at any moment and it did.

Convulsions, followed by more gasps, put me into panic mode. With trembling hands, coupled with a rapid heartfelt, I nervously and prayerfully held onto Lori and rocked her in my arms and after several minutes of crying and gasping, praying and pleading, Lori died, right there in my arms.

Spending almost a week in Mrs. Mosley's basement brought me closer to God, and to my Mom, even at that young age, I was fully aware of their presence in my life. And it was only by the grace of God that I was able to leave that basement alive.

"Anyone down there?" a raspy, deep-throated voice yelled as I saw light creeping through as the door opened.

With all the strength I could muster, I yelled, "I'm here!" as I got up. My hands lead the way through the darkness as I found my way to the stairs. My weak legs trembled at the knees while climbing.

"I'm coming! I'm Alicia!" I yelled as I moved closer to the light of day.

"Come on chile. Come on," the stranger with the raspy voice spoke as he reached out his hand to grab mine.

❧ ❧ ❧ ❧ ❧

Freedom humbly greeted my heart as I watched the cops take Mrs. Mosley away. Something about the sight of seeing that woman losing her freedom made me realize my freedom that much more. As I laid on the stretcher, the EMT, a small oriental man carefully placed me into the ambulance. Before entering the ambulance, my eyes focused on those children who became my sisters and brothers, and as I began to drift in and out of consciousness I wondered if I'd ever see them again.

A familiar voice greeted me on the ride to the hospital, and as I looked up, I would see the man who saved my life. His cocoa-enriched hand gently caressed my face. I smiled, "Are you the man who got me out of the basement?"

His smile warmed my insides, I remember, as he looked deep into my eyes with his deep, dark brown eyes. His salt and pepper hair and mustache to match made this stranger, my hero, look like what I always imagined my Dad to be. Many nights, I prayed for a strong man to call my Dad, one that would rescue me if I ever came across harm's way, a man like this stranger who just saved my life.

"Yes, I am the man. My name is Reverend Joseph Smith. Nice to meet you."

I exhaled, "Nice to meet you, too."

"You're a strong girl. You know that?"

"Yes, I'm strong like my Mom."

"Is that right?"

"Yes."

'Where is your Mom?"

"She died while giving birth to me."

"I'm sorry to hear that."

"Don't be. God told me that she is in a better place. I will get to see her soon, I'm sure of it."

"You know God, young lady?"

"I think so."

"I'm sure you do."

"Didn't God send you to save my life?"

With that same warm, endearing and comforting smile, Reverend Smith acknowledged and confirmed my assumption. "Yes, He did."

"I'm glad you did. Thank you," I smiled, then closed my eyes.

෴ ෴ ෴ ෴ ෴

The days had gone by slowly as I recovered at the medical center. And with each passing day, I was greeted by that wonderful stranger who entered and saved my life. He'd come and visit at the same time, around noon, and have lunch with me. I had grown so attached to him. I wanted him to my Dad. On one afternoon in particular, I remember asking if he would be.

"So, Reverend Smith, are you my new Dad?" I asked as I sat up in my hospital bed. The clean pajamas provided by the staff were the most comfortable pajamas I'd ever felt. Actually, I had no idea what pajamas were until I was admitted, cleaned, and my treatment for dehydration, neglect and abuse began.

"No, Alicia, I'm not your new Dad," he smiled and leaned in to rub my hand with his. I remember admiring his fashionable sweaters and how they tugged so slightly at his bulging belly.

"Why not?"

"Well, it's complicated. But the important thing is that I'm here for you and want to help you in any way I can. Now, Alicia, can you tell me if you have any siblings?"

"What?"

"Siblings. Brothers or sisters?"

"Oh. When I was at Mrs. Mosley's house, I did hear her say something about me having sisters. And I heard her speak about my Mom. She spoke to someone about my Mother. I heard that she was a writer, a singer and she was a waitress and that she died when I was born, because my Dad beat her."

"I see."

"Well, Alicia, you're going to be getting out of the hospital soon. And I want to leave you with this here," he revealed as he gave me his business card and a pamphlet on his church.

"Thank you."

"I want you to come to church every Sunday so that I can keep an eye on you."

"Okay, but where am I going after I leave the hospital?"

"You'll be going to another foster home."

When Reverend Smith spoke those words, the wind was knocked out of me, and the fear, that heart-wrenching fear that consumed me whole almost every day of my existence, terrified my spirit and I wanted my life to end. The tears that poured fluidly and relentlessly from my eyes were almost uncontrollable as Reverend Smith reached in, to hug me and console me. The soft, fuzzy sweater rubbed against my face and the smell of his cologne penetrated my senses. I knew I wanted Reverend Smith to be in my life forever and I couldn't understand why God wouldn't make him my Dad.

"There, there, young lady," he said as he patted my back, "we are going to get through this. You have to trust and believe."

Pulling away from me, Reverend Smith grabbed some tissue off of my nightstand and handed it to me. I pat my eyes dry, and wiped my paper that laid on the table where the nurse would bring my food.

"What's that you have there?"

"Oh, nothing Reverend Smith, just something I was working on."

"Like what?"

"Some poetry."

Is that right? May I hear?"

"Sure. I wrote this poem for Mrs. Mosley. Well, not really for her, more like how I imagined her life to be if she ever stopped being so mean to her children.

"I would like to hear it, Alicia," Reverend Smith commanded. I had his undivided attention.

"Okay, I'll read it to you now."

"I'm all ears."

I was passed around from one pusher to the next. I often prayed for Mrs. Mosley. Prayed that she'd get her life together. I imagined her a changed woman; a woman who would give her soul to God and let him move mountains in her life. My imagination flooded journal entries and with the gift of the written and spoken word my Mother passed down to me, I wrote and prayed for her.

"She was a pitiful soul.

Oh, what a pitiful soul.

Walking down that pitiful road.

Looking for someone just as pitiful as she.

She guessed, because misery loves company.

While wallowing in self-pity, she was sinking.

Sinking.

Could be because of the drinking, smoking, whoring.

She reached rock bottom.

Maybe even lower than that.

She had been there, done that.

Seen this, saw that.

Elissa Gabrielle

Oh yes,
Momma was a rollin' stone.
Believe me,
where she laid her hat was her home.
Drawn into ghetto madness.
The devil led her there.
Only to end up soaked in sadness.
Life,
it didn't matter, you see.
Take advantage.
Snatched all that she could get to benefit she.
Selfishly.
It didn't bother she.
No courage to think of another.
She couldn't see.
Her vision was blurry.

You see,
the crack took her there.
To the bottomless ditch she was
slowly creeping in.
Like running 100 miles an hour
into a brick wall fast.
The cocaine led the way.
Kept calling.
Made her want to live just one more day.
The pipe was her comforter,

her hero, her lover.
Her kids: "Don't worry, momma will
feed ya, as soon as I'm feeling good."
When the heroin cools.

Then came the
Triumph of the soul.
DYFS took the kids away.
No place to live.
No where to stay.
No little ones to hold tight, when she
was doing alright.
"Hey, Devil, Where you at?!
When she need to get her kids back!
You always around,
When she was foolishly behaving like
a clown."
Court gesturing.
Forever missing.

Then one day,
someone called her name.
"Get your act together, girl,
before it's too late."
She heard this so many times before.
Time and time again.
But this time it was different.
The one who was talking,

seemed to be a true friend.
It was our lord and savior Jesus Christ.
And after she accepted him,
She knew things would be alright.
Her heart opened wide.
Tears of joy rolled
from her eyes.
You see,
Our friend led her the way.
Gave her sight.
Got her kids back.
Life, it's alright.
Rising at sunrise is her plight.

The triumph of the soul
was here.
It had arrived.
Took forever to get there!
And now she is covered by the blood.
What a tender, precious love.
What a forgiving heart our friend had for she.
Allowing her the freedom to truly be happy.
The Triumph of The Soul.
And what a triumph it is.
Thank you friend,
Her Kids will see her live."

I looked up after reading my piece to Reverend Smith to find
him teary-eyed.

"I'm so proud of you, Alicia. You're a strong girl. For someone so young, you surely are very mature."

"I have to be."

"Why is that?"

"I don't know, just have to be."

"How do you know the Lord so well?"

"Believe or not Reverend Smith, every foster home I was in, I found a Bible or would hear my foster Mom talk about God, or would get dragged to church for the show of it. I watched the way people behaved in church, how they would be so happy, so I paid attention. I knew something in that church, and something about that Bible gave people joy. Since I spent most of my life being sad, I held on to the joy the Bible and church gave me. And when we stopped going to church, I always had my Bible hidden in a safe place. I would keep my writings in there too."

"Alicia, you're certainly blessed. By the way, Alicia, Mrs. Mosley is going to jail for what she did to you, the little girl Lori and the rest of the children, including her own, who were in her care. My church tries to help the children who are abused and neglected, and that's how we found out about Mrs. Mosley, which ultimately led to me finding you."

"I'm sure glad you did."

"Me too, Alicia."

๕ ๕ ๕ ๕ ๕

"Congregation, I want you to know how good God is. Amen?"

"Amen!" the congregation yelled back in unison.

"Beloveds, I want to take this time to acknowledge someone very special in my life. His name is Reverend Joseph Smith, and I'm here to tell you all, this man saved my life! I was a lonely little girl, who had been abused, neglected, molested and harmed in every way, and one day, out of the darkness, this man, my hero saved my life. Reverend Smith was sent from God to save me, and now I am here to tell you how good God is. Amen?"

"Amen!" the congregation once again yelled in joy.

With my purple and white minister's robe on, I move away from the podium, and step down the stairs to move in closer to the members of my church. With microphone in hand, and the hair my Mom passed down to me, gliding over my shoulders, I conclude my sermon for this Sunday.

"It is because of you, Reverend Smith," I point in his direction, "that I am here today. Congregation, do you know how good God is?"

"Yes!" they screamed overjoyed.

"Reverend Smith doesn't know this but I have a surprise for him today," I admit and see the Reverend smile.

"See, when Reverend Smith saved my life, he discovered that I had a gift. The gift of the spoken and written word. It was handed down to me from my Mother. And although I never met my Mother, I knew her, deep down in my soul, I knew that beautiful woman. So as a dedication to Reverend Smith, I want to share with him, a poem I wrote after I found my sweet victory."

As I move closer to Reverend Smith, I glance over my congregation and admire the beautiful members of my church, as they sit on the mahogany pews, some crying tears of joy, while others stand to their feet and praise the Lord.

"It is because of you, Reverend Smith, that I found my peace in the midst of the storm."

"In your name I pray of thee.
Comfort me, Oh Lord, comfort me.
Guide me through this chaos and despair.

In my trials and my woes,
your love provides the strength to go on.
For you are the light and my only salvation.
A precious, tender love helps battle my temptation.
Lead me the right way.
Help all of us who are torn.
For you are the Peace in the Storm.

Needed like a bible to a preacher.
With your grace, Lord, I know you can reach us.
Those who know you are here.
Those who guess, but need a boost to get there.
Those who just don't care.
Those who believe, "Life, well, It ain't worth going on."
Be our Peace in the Storm.

Wanted like shelter to a homeless child.
Bring us the beauty of the sunshine.
Light the way, give us sight.

Show me the sunlight at any time.
From the second,
the minute,
the day my child was born,
Thank you.
There is Peace in the Storm.

In the times of gloom.
We are lifted, Lord,
by the flowers you make bloom.
How magnificent you are to me
and my family.
Giving us the courage and power to be set free.
Precious one, remove from my side, this thorn.
Be my Peace in the Storm.

I walk by faith.
And acknowledge that the gift of sight
does not come from the eyes that you have bestowed upon
me.
But only from the miracle that is you.
The miracle that is me.
For I am here, breathing.
With a heart beating
and walking feet.

Dear Spirit, look after me.

Teacher, please guide and comfort me.
My Spirit, my Lord set free.
As I am here to serve thee.
Be with me through these trying times.
Shield me from the evils that lurk in the night.
Have mercy on my soul, dear Lord.
My Peace in the Storm."

Reverend Smith rises to his feet, and still sharp as a tack, he sobs, a deep, thankful and joyful sob, and as I move closer to him, the congregation praises the Lord.

I reach out my hand to take his, the same way he'd done for me those many years ago. Hand in hand, I speak to my congregation hoping to reach them all through my message of triumph over adversity.

"People, I want you to know one thing today as you go on your way. Know under no uncertain terms that God wants you to have the victory. You are significant.

Your essence establishes a difference. No matter what others may say to you, think of you or do to you, God loves you. Amen?"

"Amen!"

"Believe that all things are possible. Let trust and faith keep you alive. Reverend Smith witnessed the triumph of my soul, now let me witness yours. Do you know how good God is?"

"Yes!"

In Loving Memory

Stanley S. James
Frances Barnes

The contributing authors of The Triumph of My Soul
would love to hear from you.
Please visit us online at
www.TheTriumphOfMySoul.com
and email the authors at
Anthology@TheTriumphOfMySoul.com.

The Triumph Of My Soul

Ordering Information

Yes! Please send me _____ copies of
The Triumph Of My Soul.
ISBN-13: 978-0-9790222-2-7 | ISBN-10: 0-9790222-2-3

Please include $16.00 plus $3.00 shipping/handling for
the first book, and $1.00 for each additional book.

Send my book(s) to:

Name:_____

Address:_____

City, State, Zip:_____

Telephone:_____

Email:_____

Would you like to receive emails from Elissa Gabrielle?
_____Yes   _____No

Make checks and money orders payable to Elissa Gabrielle.

The Triumph Of My Soul
Attn: Book Orders
P.O. Box 1152
Pocono Summit, PA 18346

Visit on the web:

www.TheTriumphOfMySoul.com

Printed in the United States
107004LV00003B/46-93/A

9 780979 022227